Tactical Inferno

Copyright

Paperback ISBN: 978-1-961966-14-7

Published by: Carxander Publishing
Minnesota

Disclaimer

The books in this series are based completely on dreams that I've had or that one of the other people in my relationship has had. They all have a little bit of real life thrown in so that you, the reader, can get to know us a little bit better.

These books can and should be read as standalone books. There isn't an order to them. All of the characters in the books are the same, as they are all based on characters from real life.

As you read these books, please keep in mind that other than the characters and the city they are based in, these books are not connected to other books in the series. They aren't a continuation of other books. They are all novellas based on dreams that revolve around the same characters.

As you keep that in mind, please enjoy reading this book. I do hope you will also read the others in this series and love them as much as I loved writing them!

Opening Quote

For a moment like this. Some people wait a lifetime for a moment like this. Some people search forever for that one special kiss. Oh, I can't believe it's happening to me. Some people wait a lifetime for a moment like this. Could this be the greatest love of all? I wanna know that you will catch me when I fall.

A Moment Like This by Kelly Clarkson

Chapter One

☆ Mariah ☆

I pause my music and sigh as I take one headphone out of my ear. I seriously contemplate not answering the phone, but I know it would be fruitless. Tyler Alexander, my agent, would certainly just show up at my doorstep.

Ever since I signed with Alexander's Publishing House, I've been treated like royalty. I don't understand why. I'm an author. I write romance novels for a living. Apparently, though, my first book sounded like a winner to them. It hit the bestseller's list right away. They knew they had a sure thing with me.

Lucky for them, I had an entire series completed before I had even gone to them. They were ecstatic. I'm still humbled that my name generates so much hype. I get to do what I love while they make a lot of money. It's a win-win for us all.

I sigh again as I answer the phone. "Hello?"

"Mariah. It's Tyler." His deep voice probably brings women to their knees.

He's certainly attractive enough to have women lining up at his door. Tall, dirty blond hair, clean-shaven, and muscular. He looks as good in jeans as he does in his suit. I've been with him and seen women drool over him. I can see the appeal, but he's not my type. Not like he hasn't tried once or twice. Tyler is my best-friend, though. One of the two people in the world I've ever truly let in.

"I know, Tyler. This is the twenty-first century. I have a Caller ID. Your name very graciously pops up on my phone's screen as Pain in my Ass." I smirk.

He laughs low and deep. Rich. Powerful. As it should. He's the son of the man in charge of the publishing house. His father, Baron Alexander, assigned him to work with me directly after my first book became their top-selling novel of all time.

"Good to know. Though, you say that like I didn't already. I'm just checking in."

I raise an eyebrow. "You mean you want to know when you're getting the first draft."

He chuckles. "Sure. That, too. Mostly, I am really just checking in. I miss talking to you. But since we're on the subject of the book, you do have a deadline."

I sigh because I have the draft he wants. I've just been leery about submitting it. "I don't know, Tyler. I…" I rub my forehead.

He pauses and sighs. "Please tell me you aren't having writer's block or whatever the hell you all call it."

I glare at the phone before putting it back to my ear. "Sometimes, you can be an asshole."

"It's why I'm so good at my job. And why they assigned me to you. Something about giving you only the best." There's so much cockiness and definitely a smirk in his voice.

"I have it, but I really don't know how it's going to be taken."

"Come on. You can't be serious. You know how beloved your writing is. Your books fly off the shelves. And I'm not just saying that because I'm your agent."

I slump slightly. "I can't argue with you, Tyler, but people are used to heterosexual romance from me. Sexy. Male and female. Panty-soaking and dick-hardening sex scenes. This is… different."

Tyler is quiet a few moments before he takes a deep breath. "More personal."

My eyes widen, and I choke on my own spit. I start coughing. There's no way he could know that. No way at all. I haven't told anyone my secret. I've nearly told him several times, but I don't want him to think differently of me. I've only told one person. It's a secret I've kept very close to my heart since I was a teenager. Probably sooner than that even. There's no possible way he could know that this book is more personal.

More... me.

I rub my throat when I regain myself. "What?"

"Mariah, you and I have been working together for years. If you honestly think I didn't know, you have another thing coming. I'm like your fucking brother."

I blink a few times, dumbfounded. "I've been so careful about it. How do you know?"

He chuckles. "I'm just very intuitive. And I know you. If it makes you feel better, your secret is safe with me. My father has no idea. But I get the feeling he's about to if what you're getting at is what I think it is."

I smile softly and chuckle as I shake my head. "I think one of the reasons we get along is because you cut right through the bullshit. I like that you don't mess around."

"I'm happy you feel that way. Now. Talk to me about the book. I wasn't kidding about the deadline."

I pout and sigh. "It's a female with another female. It's still romance. Still steamy. Just not the typical thing I write. I'm nervous. I mean, I don't know if it will be accepted by my audience, but I really don't think Baron will like it."

"It's not your job to worry about if he'll like it. It's mine. My job is to push you and your book. Your brand. Which is steamy and spicy as fuck romance. Give me steamy and sexy, and I'll do the rest."

I relax a little. He may be a pain, but the man really does fight for me. He's the best agent anyone could ask for. I don't know what I'd do without him. He's managed to not only get me one hell of a team, but he keeps me on track, and he's even sometimes a great sounding board. Since I've only allowed two people into my world since I left my old life behind and started this journey, me admitting that he's one of my two best friends is really saying something.

"What are the chances of him kicking me out of the publishing house?" I ask with a wry chuckle.

"Slim to none. Your fans eat up your work. It doesn't matter what we put out. Your name is synonymous with sales."

"My name is synonymous with heterosexual -"

"Mariah. Fuck. I love you, but stop. Give me the first draft, or I'm flying to Gainesville to get it myself. I could use some Florida sun. After that, book that cruise you've been talking about for months. You need it."

He hangs up before I have a chance to retort. I toss my phone on the couch. "I both hate and love you, you fucker," I grumble on my way to grab my laptop.

I sigh as I sit down and open it. I quickly pull up my first draft and send it to Tyler before he makes good on his threat. Though, I would like to see him. Besides Justice, my best and only friend here, I really stay away from everyone. I don't have a social life because I don't like people. Rather, the ones who repeatedly show what horrible humans they are.

This is the entire reason I have a wolf for a pet. He loves me unconditionally and won't let anyone take me for granted. I swear, sometimes, I think his uncanny ability to sniff out bullshit is God's way of making up for everything he ever put me through. In this life and any past life I may have had.

I smile softly thinking of the cruise Tyler suggested. It's a really good idea. An all-inclusive, all lesbian cruise that goes to the Caribbeans. I've been wanting to book it for a couple of years, but I haven't been able to. Other obligations seem to keep arising. Like where to keep my wolf. Maybe this year, I'll see if my friend Justice wants to come. If I can figure out a place that will take my wolf. I can't just leave him, and I'm sure they won't let me take him on the cruise.

I close the laptop after sending the email with my first draft. Tyler will look it over before sending it to my editor. I never send it to the editor, or anyone else, without it going through Tyler. He's very protective of my work. Just as much as me. If he thinks there should be a change or something added, I trust him more than anyone, but it's because he makes sure that my work is properly protected before anyone else gets their hands on it.

I smile and giggle softly when my jet-black wolf pops his head up to look at me. His lips curl up in a quiet growl. "Don't look at me like that, Loki. I know."

He watches me a few more moments before licking his lips and putting his head down. I have an asshole for a wolf. Just as he is a good judge of character, he's also very good about keeping negative thoughts out of my head. Every time I'm just about to think about how my fans will turn on me for my story, or something equally detrimental to my mental health, he gives me a warning growl.

I stand and restlessly walk to my patio. When I moved to Gainesville almost four years ago, I fell head over heels in love with the house. The small wolf pup I had just acquired fell just as much in love with it as I did.

I wait for Loki to follow me outside. He never misses a chance to be in the backyard of our small house with me. There's lots of space for him. He's quite content here. After all I've heard about wolves as pets, I consider that a win. Apparently, they enjoy digging. They can be aggressive and don't listen because they are wild and have wild spirits. Several states in the United States have flat out banned owning wolves or wolfdogs as pets. Then again, these are the same states who have banned pit bulls. From what I've seen, if raised correctly, pit bulls are one of the most loving dogs.

I laugh when Loki foregoes his run around the yard and jumps up in the pool chair next to me. He lays down with a huff.

"What's your deal today? You're all growly and moody."

He looks at me and lays his head on my lap.

"Aww... I see." I reach down and scratch his years. "You've decided I needed some extra wolf attention."

He licks his lips and closes his eyes.

I laugh again. "Such a good boy." I continue to pet him. Loki is a big wolf. He's got a lot of muscle. I'm really not that tall, but he stands nearly to my waist on all four of his paws, which are freaking giant. He towers over me if he's on two paws.

I moved to Gainesville, Florida, just after I signed with Alexander's Publishing House. My life was insanity. My anxiety was at an all-time high. I needed to start fresh. Away from my corporate job. Away from the people who said they cared about me but didn't. But, most importantly, away from all of the assholes who pretended to be my friends but weren't. I guess when a person is forced out of a high paying job and decides to pursue their dreams, they find out really quickly who their true friends and supporters really are.

After a brief stay with Tyler in New York, I moved down here with nothing. At all. I planned to start over completely. I had a few personal items that mean the world to me, like a bracelet given to me by my grandmother, but other than that, nothing. I put myself in a hotel while I looked for a place to live. It didn't take as long as I thought. I had this house within a month.

It's really not that large. It's a one-level, two-bedroom, two-bath house. It's in a good part of town. It's got a pool, and a huge fenced-in backyard. The basement is fully furnished. It could work as another apartment or something. Instead, though, I've turned it into my place of retreat. I had a third bathroom installed. Small. Just a sink and toilet. The basement is perfect. No windows. It's almost like a cave. My own little bat-cave.

Or, I suppose, in the words of Loki, if he could talk, it's a wolf-den. He spends just as much time down there as I do. So much so, that I actually bought him one of those large dog bed things. He looked at it with disdain for an entire week before he finally tried it out. Now, he loves the hell out of it.

I lay back and let the sun do its job. It always manages to warm and relax me when I'm feeling a little out of control, cold, and dark. Of course, I'm not completely ignorant. I know that Loki is probably what brings me back the most.

I decided when I found the house, I also wanted a pet. I went to an animal rescue and looked around for a dog. That very day, though, some police officers had brought in some wolf pups. Only they all thought they were wolfdogs. They'd been brought in from a breeder who was found to be abusing his animals. A neighbor had turned him in.

It was fate. I saw Loki. He was the largest of the pups, though still small. They were all barely eight weeks old. Loki, though, was curled around the rest of them the best he could be. I wanted all of them, but I had to choose one. As soon as his chocolate eyes met mine, I knew he was the one. I don't care what anyone says. We connected.

I adopted him that very day, though they wouldn't allow me to take him. They needed to make sure everything was okay with him. As soon as they did, they processed my adoption fee and let me take him.

We've been inseparable ever since. I don't go out much, but when I do, he comes with me. Unless it's somewhere he can't be. Rare, but it happens. We both hate it.

It wasn't long after that when the center found out Loki was a purebred wolf. Not a wolfdog. They asked me if I wanted to give him back. Legally, they couldn't make me, but they understood if I wanted to. Of course, I didn't. I inquired about the other ones. They couldn't give me information on who adopted them, but assured me that they were all in a good home, and the owners, as I had, refused to give them up. That made me feel a lot better. I'm glad Loki's pack also have good homes.

I yawn and glance at my phone as Loki yawns as well. "Oh." I pick up my phone excitedly. "Hey, Justice!"

"Hey. How are you? Did you submit your book?"

I furrow my brows at her tone. She sounds sad. Melancholy almost. "I did. Tyler called and threatened to fly down here if I didn't. What's wrong?"

She sighs so sadly that my heart hurts. "It's my boyfriend. Well, my ex. Richard."

My heart sinks. "Oh... Did you two talk? What happened?"

"He didn't take it well." She sniffles.

Justice, much like me, has been fighting her true self for a long time. We met when she tripped and spilled her coffee on me. We started talking and really hit it off. After a couple of months, we felt close enough to each other to be really honest. She first admitted to me that she isn't attracted to the men who constantly hit on her. At first, I thought maybe that meant she just hadn't met the man who gets her blood boiling. But she told me she's attracted to women instead.

I'm not entirely certain I was all that surprised. I actually let out a breath and told her that I'm the same. For years, my family wondered why I had never married and had kids. Why my relationships never lasted. I had always told them I would never get married or have kids. It just wasn't in me. It wasn't in me because I am attracted to women. Only, I didn't think I could be honest about that as my reason. So, I kept it inside to avoid the frustration and stigma that comes along with being attracted to the same sex. Especially in a highly religious family.

"What happened?" I ask quietly.

She sniffles and sighs. "He said if I wanted to break up with him, I could have come up with a better reason. Something about if I really was into girls then he wouldn't have been able to make me come."

"Well, that's completely ridiculous. Having an orgasm has nothing to do with attraction. It's all scientifical. Just because he happens to be one of the only men in the world who knows where to touch a woman to make her come doesn't have anything to do with it."

She sadly chuckles. "He doesn't see it that way." She pauses. "I found out some things about him, too. I was hoping I could talk to you."

I rub my forehead. I don't know why that doesn't surprise me. Richard is sketchy as fuck to me. "Why don't you come over? I'll order a pizza. We can talk about how crappy men are and all the reasons we prefer women."

That gets a laugh out of her. "Mariah! You're awful."

I smile. "I'll even throw in chicken wings. And bruschetta flatbread."

"Add ravioli Frita. We can truly pig out. I'll be there in twenty."

"Done."

I smile as I hang up because she's laughing. I instantly call our favorite pizza delivery. No one can beat Piesanos. Their pizzas are incredible. Melt in my mouth goodness. But it's the bruschetta flatbread that makes me love them so much. That and the ravioli Frita is capable of bringing the strongest of souls to their knees.

An hour later, when the food arrives, I'm a little baffled and worried why Justice isn't here. I call her a second time, after calling her twenty minutes ago when I first started to worry, and am immediately more uneasy when it goes directly to her voicemail. I wait for the beep and look down at Loki.

"Hey, Justice. Food is here. I'm pretty worried you aren't. Give me a call, okay? I'm hoping you're just stuck in traffic."

Three hours later, though, she's still not here, and I'm pacing. The food has long gone cold, but I could care less. I've called several times now. She hasn't returned my calls or texts. It's so unlike her, I've nearly called the police.

I sigh after putting my phone down. I take a breath. "I'm going over there. She should have been here a long time ago. There's no way she wouldn't call me if she could."

Loki gives a chuff in agreement and leads me to the door. I've gotten pretty good at reading him since I've had him. Loki is nervous. His fur around his neck seems to be standing up. I've learned to trust my wolf. He never plays off my anxiety and becomes anxious or agitated himself. If he's freaked out, he has a reason to be.

I quickly grab my keys and run out the door, Loki just ahead of me. We make our way to my car and waste no time making the short drive to Justice's house. It's only twenty-minutes away. As I turn into her driveway, the sight in front of me makes me tilt my head.

Her car is still in the garage. Her garage door is up. Justice never leaves her garage door open. She never leaves the light in the garage on if she's not in it. I don't see her, but the light is on. I slowly get out of the car. Loki jumps out after me and moves himself in front of me. He's immediately on alert. His ears stand straight. He sniffs the air as he looks around.

"Loki? What is it?"

He growls low and walks warily towards the house on high alert. I follow him and look around as I hug myself. The hairs on the back of my neck are standing up. Those on my arms are definitely at attention. Something is wrong. There's no denying it.

When Loki gets to the door, I take a breath. I knock. After a few moments, there's no answer. I knock again, louder this time. After another few moments, there's still no answer. Everything sounds silent.

Deathly silent.

I knock once more. "Justice? It's me. Mariah," I call out as loudly as I dare. My voice sounds squeaky and terrified even to my own ears.

When she, once again, doesn't answer, I take a couple of steps away from the door. Thinking she might be in the back and not hear me, I start heading towards the gate that leads around the house. Loki immediately takes the lead, though. The fact that he's so on edge and protective is scaring me more and more.

I become more anxious when I see the gate leading to the backyard is open. Loki walks through slowly, glancing back to make sure I'm behind him. I hug myself tighter. I've never felt more apprehensive about anything in my life as I do right now. I've never been more grateful for Loki. I know if anything jumps out, I have him.

"Justice?" I call again.

I swear to God Loki glares at me as he snaps his head towards me. He chuffs in warning. I shut my mouth instantly. He silently walks around the corner. I don't know why, but I wait. I don't know if I'm waiting for him to signal me. Or if I'm waiting to be attacked. Whatever it is, I don't move.

When Loki looks at me and starts moving again, I follow him. I'm hugging myself so tightly, I'm not sure how I'm still able to breathe. Loki stops once more and sits. He's looking inside the house. I dread what I'm about to do, but I force my eyes off my wolf and follow his gaze.

My heart ceases to beat.

My lungs stop taking in air.

My knees collapse under me, and I fall in a heap to the ground.

The kitchen floor is covered in a pool of darkening fluid. There is a large butcher knife also coated in the substance. I recognize it from the set I got her for her birthday last year. The handles are customized with a dragon, her favorite mythical creature. The dark liquid is spreading across the hardwood onto the white carpet of her living room.

I swear I hear screaming, even though I see no other soul around but Loki. I want to look away, but I can't. It takes Loki standing in front of me for me to realize the high-pitched sound of terror is coming from me.

I bury my face in his fur, screaming and crying, while I try to get my phone out of my pocket. I know I need to call someone. I try to crawl towards the house, but Loki stops me with a sharp bark and dangerous growl that stops me in my tracks. He physically pushes me back gently, not allowing me to enter the house.

Unable to stop screaming and crying, I dial 911. The voice on the other end grows more and more distant the longer I stare in horror at the gore in front of me.

Chapter Two

☆ Lyric ☆

"Squad twelve and twenty-seven," a male voice from our dispatch says over the radio.

"Go ahead," I answer.

"Go for twenty-seven," Lieutenant Matt Chance's deep and powerful voice responds.

"Call at a residential home. I sent the address to you. RP is very hard to understand. She's screaming. All I can get out of her is send help. She's bleeding. I don't know who is bleeding, but she did say it isn't her. I have EMT on the way."

I sigh. None of that sounds good. Not that any calls we get are necessarily good. Police respond to calls for help and service to people who are having their worst days. But any call that comes in where someone is screaming, not able to give much information, and there is blood involved is bound to become a bad day for us. Not as bad as the victim and their family, but still bad.

"10-4," I say as I scan the address on my squad's laptop. "Huh." I furrow my brows. "That's a really good neighborhood."

I head towards the address and smile softly to myself as I drive at Code Three, lights and sirens as quickly as possible, through the city I call home. Ever since I was a kid, I wanted to move to the United States from my home country of the United Kingdom. I never felt like I belonged there. It was never truly home. Five years ago, I followed my heart and my dreams. I jumped on a plane with my belongings and flew to the United States.

Gainesville, Florida, is where I made my home. Something about the liveliness of the town drew me in. It's a college town. There's always something to do. Plays. Concerts. Clubs. Tons of different kinds of restaurants.

But the draw for me was how accepting the city is to people like me. The small city I came from is nothing but one big clique. Same-sex relationships, while not banned, are frowned upon. So much so that one of my friends who came out to her family was disowned and chased, more or less, to London. A larger city with more idealistic beliefs and greater acceptance, but far too large for me.

Here, in Gainesville, I've been able to be myself and express myself. I've even had relationships, though none of them lasted, with other women. It's something I couldn't do in Hertfordshire.

So, I moved. I started a new life around new people who accepted me for who I am. And I followed another dream. Becoming a cop. It's been a busy five years, but so incredibly rewarding. I just turned thirty-one and feel like I've accomplished so much in my life I didn't have a prayer of accomplishing in the United Kingdom.

I arrive to the house behind Matt. He's both my friend and the Lieutenant working today. He doesn't get out on the streets too often, but we both love when he's able to. Today, he's taken over for my usual partner, who is out on vacation.

I step out of my squad as Matt does. Matt is tall. He's six feet four. He's built very well. He has short dark hair and dark brown eyes to go with his broody features. If he weren't wearing a uniform, I'm not sure many people would peg him for a cop. He has a sleeve tattoo covering his left arm. A cross, rosary beads, roses, and a bunch of other things that are uniquely Matt. He even has tattoos on his right arm. His face has scruff. Not enough to be considered a beard by any means. He's not at all unkempt. Just not how people envision a cop when they think of one.

Matt looks down at me when I reach him. "Not wearing a jacket?"

I rub my arms. It's pitch-black out. The sun set a long time ago, and it's chilly. Not something people think of when they think of Florida. "I left it in my locker. I was on my way back to get it when the call came in."

Matt nods and pops his trunk. He ruffles in his gym bag and pulls out a long-sleeve shirt. "Put this over the long-sleeve shirt you have on. Take off your uniform shirt. Hurry up. I'm going to head the house."

My eyes widen. "Not without back-up you aren't. You don't know what you're walking into."

Matt points over my shoulder. "Captain Rens just showed up. Hurry up."

I smile at the mention of Matt's husband, DJ Rens. Like Matt, he's tall. He's only about an inch shorter than Matt. But he's just as built. Just as dark and broody. His eyes, though, are a beautiful shade of green.

I was over the moon when they got married a couple of years ago. It was an incredible thing for me to see. Two people in love who are the same sex gave me hope that I, too, could find the type of relationship they have and live my happily ever after.

I quickly put Matt's long-sleeve shirt on while he and DJ walk up to the house. I watch them as they clear the garage. By the time they start walking to the back of the house, I'm hot on their heels. We all have our guns drawn because we have no idea what's really going on.

"Holy shit," Matt says as he stops short.

My eyes widen when I hear a low growl. Dangerous. Protective. I watch as Matt slowly kneels down. DJ keeps his gun aimed at whatever growled. I follow his lead as I slowly move to his side. In front of us is a large, black wolf sitting in front of a woman who has curled into herself. She's gripping his fur. Her body is trembling. It doesn't take much to see she's crying. I glance at DJ for direction.

"Keep trained on the wolf," DJ says barely above a whisper without looking at me.

I follow his command without hesitation. The wolf bares his teeth with a low growl once more, sending my heart rate skyrocketing. If he were to decide we're a threat to the woman he's guarding, I'm not sure we'd have a chance of taking him out before he seriously injured us. It's not something I would ever want to do. I have a wolf for a pet. It's for that reason alone that I know exactly how protective they are.

I take a breath. Matt and DJ also have wolves. The three of us adopted a pack of wolves a few years ago that we took from a breeder who was mistreating his animals. There were four wolf pups. We were told one of them had been adopted. I can't help but wonder if this is that wolf pup. I remember he was black.

Matt puts his gun away, trusting that we have his back. He holds out a hand to the wolf. "Hey, there, boy." His voice has lost all the commanding edge we're all used to. The wolf, however, doesn't give a crap. He growls just as dangerously. "I don't blame you. Three people you don't know around your person. But we're here to help. I promise. We're not going to hurt you or her."

"Loki," a sweet and broken voice cracks.

"Loki," Matt says. "I have a wolf, too, boy. I understand how protective you are." Matt, still kneeling, takes a couple of steps closer. He makes certain that not only is the wolf in his line of sight, but also the back of the house.

"Matt," I whisper, shakily, as the wolf sniffs the air.

Matt nods, acknowledging my warning but saying nothing to me. "Good boy. You can sense the wolf on me, huh?" He takes a couple slow steps closer, still being mindful of the back of the house. The wolf whines. "See? I'm the good guy."

The woman slowly lifts her head. Despite her tear-soaked cheeks and puffy red eyes, she's the most beautiful woman I've ever seen. Her hair is a long dark brown. She's small. She can't be taller than me. I'm five feet four. She's wearing distressed jeans and a pink tank top that shows off her perfect curves. I have to shake my head to regain my composure.

"It's o-okay, Loki," she says quietly as she soothingly pets him, though her hand is as shaky as her voice. "He's the p-police. He's here t-to help."

Matt reaches them both, still keeping his hand outstretched. Loki sniffs it cautiously before nuzzling it with his head. "Good boy. Protecting mama. Think we can talk to her?" Matt nods towards the woman. Loki rumbles but doesn't leave the woman's side. "Lyric? Stay with Loki and Ms…?" Matt looks at the woman but doesn't move.

"C-Carter," she whispers.

"Ms. Carter. See what happened. DJ and I will take the house. Sound okay to you, Loki?" He ruffles Loki's head as he stands. Loki rumbles as if he's agreeing with him.

I cautiously approach Loki and Ms. Carter but don't put my gun away. If DJ and Matt intend on entering the house, I need to be ready in case someone runs out of it. Loki watches my every move just as carefully as I watch his. Ms. Carter buries her face back into her wolf's fur. As I watch DJ and Matt enter the house, announcing themselves as the police with their guns drawn, I can see exactly why the wolf is guarding her.

Laying on the ground in a pool of blood is a woman. What I think is blond hair is darkened by the fluid. It's spread around her head and looks to be sticking to the floor. In the darkened fluid on the floor is a knife covered in blood.

"Oh God," I whisper as I cover my mouth.

I've been a police officer here in Gainesville for a few years. I haven't responded to a call of anyone dead. I know I've been lucky. But as I stare at the horror of the scene in front of me, I want to cry. Tears sting my eyes. I barely hear DJ's voice over the radio calling our Homicide Investigations team in.

I try to hold myself together, but I feel a tear trickle down my cheek. I wipe it away and try to keep my focus on the house instead of the scene. Matt and DJ need me to cover them and watch the woman who just became a suspect.

"What happened?" I ask her. The shaky quiver in my voice betrays the strength I'm trying to portray.

"This is how sh-she was when I g-got h-here." She hiccups and sniffles, hugging Loki.

"Wait." I shake my head. "I have to Mirandize you."

"I know," she whispers.

I glance down at her then focus on the house again. "You have the right to remain silent," I begin, reciting the warning I know by heart. "Anything you say can and will be used against you in the Court of Law. You have the right to an attorney. If you can't afford one, one will be appointed to you by the Court. Do you understand these rights as I have read them to you?"

She sniffles. "I understand my r-rights, Officer."

"Having these rights in mind, do you wish to talk to me at this time?"

"Yes, ma'am. I'll a-answer your questions."

I watch as Matt and DJ appear back in my sight. They clear the scene over the radio and cancel the medics, instead calling for a coroner. I breathe a slight sigh of relief knowing the house doesn't have anyone waiting to jump them, but I'm still on edge because whoever did this could be anywhere right now. They could be coming back. It could be the woman curled into a giant wolf at my feet. Though, instincts tell me she's not the one who did this.

"She was s-supposed to come over to my h-house for dinner. She broke up with h-her boyfriend today. She's b-een struggling to tell him that sh-she…" She takes a deep breath and sniffles again. "She's not attracted to him. She's a-attracted to women. I guess he didn't t-take it too well."

Keeping an eye on my partners and our surrounding area, I put my gun away and take out my small notebook. "Do you know his name?"

"Richard." She wipes her eyes. Loki stays where he is, blocking her view of the travesty in front of her. "McAdams."

I nod. "Do you know anything about him? Where he lives? Works?"

She looks up at me. She looks broken. Her hazel eyes look dull and lifeless. "He's an attorney," she whispers. She looks back in front of her and focuses on her wolf's fur. "At least that's what he said he was. We… had our doubts."

I raise an eyebrow and look down at her. "What do you mean?"

She takes a breath. "Well, he drove a really nice car, but said he didn't get a lot of cases." She shrugs. "Lots of things didn't add up. Justice was coming to my house be-cause sh-she found something she w-wanted to talk about."

I'm about to question her further, but Matt and DJ both come outside talking in hushed tones as they focus on Ms. Carter. I watch them both curiously as they stop in front of us and quit talking. She looks up at them.

DJ clears his throat. "Ms. Carter, I need to ask you to stand up, please. We'd like to ask you some questions, but we'd prefer to do it downtown. You're not under arrest. We'd just like to question you about what happened here in peace. This scene is about to get chaotic when everyone shows up."

Ms. Carter stands slowly. "What about Loki?" she whispers.

Matt kneels in front of him. Loki licks his face as he pets him. "I'm sure Loki would love to go for a ride. He can hang out in my office."

She just nods. The detectives start showing up. DJ turns and starts commanding the scene. He's a Captain for the investigations team. He doesn't often go on patrol, but when he's bored, he'll jump in a squad. It's one of the reasons everyone respects him so much. He's never forgotten, or allowed himself to forget, the streets.

Ms. Carter hugs herself. She looks like she's about to fall over. All I want to do is be the one to give her the comfort she so desperately seeks. I can see the goosebumps along her skin. She has to be freezing. The wind is a little chilly and damp, but the temperature has dropped several degrees since the sun went down. It has to be in the forties. I'm wearing two long sleeve shirts and still feel chilled.

"Maybe we could get her to her car?" I ask Matt. "She could follow us."

Matt shakes his head. "I don't think she's in the right state of mind to drive. A gust of wind could blow her over."

Ms. Carter chuckles weakly. "You're probably right," she says softly. She wipes her eyes. "Aren't I a suspect? Shouldn't I be in handcuffs?"

"You have no blood on your clothing. None in your hair. None on your hands," Matt says. "But what's more is there are bloody shoe prints all throughout the house. And they are way too big to belong to you. Captain Rens ruled you out as a suspect as soon as we walked into the house. That is a crime of passion." Matt gestures over his shoulder.

Ms. Carter breathes out a long sigh. I don't know if it's relief, or if she's upset by what Matt said. Probably both. I can't really blame her. This scene isn't easy for me, and I'm paid to deal with it. She's just a bystander who reported it. At least that's what the evidence here suggests.

"Let's get you to a squad," I say softly. She takes a few steps but looks as if she might collapse. I quickly put an arm around her as she stumbles. "I got you."

I inhale sharply and quietly as soon as my arm snakes around her waist. I firmly grip her hip to keep her from falling, but it's hard to ignore the bolt of electricity that seems to shoot through me. The feeling I've never managed to feel with anyone. I thought it was just me. I thought I was destined to walk this Earth alone, never finding my one true love.

Not that I haven't been with other women. I have. But it's always been superficial. Something we both knew going into it wouldn't last. It was nothing more than a sexual relief. Leave it to me to finally feel that special something with a woman I met while on what turned out to be a murder call.

I bite my lip to keep myself grounded and not get lost against the feel of her silky skin under my fingertips from where her tank top slightly rose up. Her soft curves have the ability to drive anyone crazy. I'm not immune to her anymore than anyone would be.

But I do have a job to do. A job I take very seriously. I don't even know if she's attracted to women. I know nothing about her at all. I don't even know her first name. I don't know what she saw. I don't know how she's involved.

I sigh when we reach my squad. "I just need to pat you down," I say quietly. "For my safety and yours. You don't have anything on you that will poke or stick me, do you?"

She shakes her head slowly. "Just my phone," she whispers. She's tired. I can hear it in her voice. "In my back pocket. My driver's license and some cash are in the case."

I nod as Matt and DJ watch me. I pat her down, trying not to linger anywhere too long. Trying not to sink in her sexy coconut and coffee with a hint of vanilla scent. I bite back a groan at my wayward, very unprofessional, and stupidly ridiculous thoughts. I need to get a hold of myself. Quickly.

After patting her down, I help her into the backseat of my squad. She slides over so Loki can jump in beside her. I close the door and take a deep, cleansing breath. It doesn't work. I shake my head before turning around. DJ and Matt are both watching me.

They know.

Assholes.

"Not... a... word..." I glare at them both as they laugh and head for their squads. I growl low because they know me far too well for my liking right now. I walk around to the driver's side of my car before a realization strikes me. "DJ, aren't you supposed to run the scene?" I call to him before he ducks into his squad.

He shrugs and grins. "Good thing about being a Captain is delegation. We have a rapport going with her. I'll take questioning while they investigate. They need me, they know where to find me." He ducks into his squad car.

I can't help but chuckle a little, but the truth is I'm really glad that he's decided to question Ms. Carter. The idea of one of the other detectives doing it bothers me. DJ is one of my best friends. I know he'll be gentle with the questioning, and I really think she needs that.

I don't know why I care so much so quickly about her. Maybe it's my heart. I've always been told I get emotionally attached quickly to people. I've always thought I have trust issues, but maybe I trust too easily.

As I follow Matt back to the station, though, I glance in the rearview mirror. Ms. Carter is, once again, burrowed into the fur of her massive wolf. Loki is standing guard over her. I chew on the inside of my cheek and focus back on the road. My mind wanders to just a few minutes ago when I was helping her to my squad.

Maybe it was just wishful thinking on my part, but I swear I heard her gasp slightly at my touch. I can't get the quiet sound out of my head. As I glance back in the mirror again, I think to myself…

Did she feel it, too?

Chapter Three

☆ *Mariah* ☆

I snuggle the wool blanket around me more and sigh. Loki is curled at my feet in the small, cold room of Gainesville Police Department's Headquarters building. I don't know how long I've been here, but it seems like forever. I look up when the door opens and Captain Rens returns with the hot drink he promised.

"I believe I owe you a latte. It's instant. Best I can do right now." He hands me a steaming mug with the GPD logo on it.

I take it and let it warm my hands. "I'd take stale coffee if it was warm." I take a tiny sip and smile as the warmness of the liquid soothes my dry throat.

Captain Rens sits down with his cup. "I appreciate you answering all the questions I've thrown at you. It's gotta be tough walking in on what you did." He sips his drink as he watches me with his cool green eyes.

"It wasn't easy," I say softly. "It's an image that I'll never get out of my head." I focus on the latte in the cup, hoping the bloody picture in my mind fades away. It doesn't. "Pretty sure I'll never sleep again, Captain Rens."

"It's DJ, Mariah. And I can't say I'd blame you if you didn't sleep again. This is something that doesn't leave a person's mind. It's traumatic." He reaches in his breast pocket and pulls out a card. "My number is on there. You can call me anytime if you need to talk. My husband and I keep long hours so we're usually available and always have our phones on. If you think of anything else, you can call."

I give him a weak smile and sip my drink. "So… what happens now?"

He leans back in his chair. "Well, the DNA we took and fingerprints for you as well as the pictures of your shoes and clothing will all rule you out as a suspect. Which we've already done. All of that was just procedural. My team back at your friend's house will gather all of the evidence they see. Probably even a lot that doesn't seem like it would matter. From there, we'll try to find the person who killed her. With what you've told me, we have a lead with her boyfriend -"

"Ex," I say as I clear my throat.

DJ smiles and nods. "Ex-boyfriend. We'll haul him in for questioning."

"I know it was him," I whisper as I sniffle. I wipe my eyes. "I know it. I've been thinking about it. Everything points to him."

"We'll pull the surveillance you said she has. I'm hoping it was on and operational, but I'm always very cautious when it comes to relying on that. A lot of times, especially if the person who did it is well-known to the victim, the surveillance is the first thing that's taken out. Hopefully, we'll get lucky."

"What if you can't find him?" I ask. "He lived with her. At least he basically did. He was there all the time, she said. If he did this…" I trail off and put my latte on the table. My hands are suddenly very shaky.

"We have lots of ways, Mariah," he says soothingly.

I look at him for a few moments. He seems so confident. I have no choice but to believe him. I let out a breath and nod as I hug myself. My mind has been racing for the past few hours. Ever since I saw Justice laying on her floor. But it keeps going back to the pretty cop. As soon as she saw the body, she seemed taken aback. Sort of like she'd never seen a dead body before. I've been worried about her. I'm curious if she's okay.

I've also been unable to stop thinking of her hand on my waist as she was helping me to her car. My tank top had come up a little. Her hand

25

was on my skin. It was warm and so soft. I'd never really felt much with anyone when they've touched me, but her… It was like a jolt. Like my blood just turned to fire or something. I've never felt anything like it.

"How's the other officer who was with you?" I ask DJ. "The girl. She seemed… really shaken."

"Lyric? She's okay. Handled it all like a trooper. She's a good girl. Good cop."

I nod slowly and shiver. "I'm glad." I fight back a yawn, but that never works. I yawn anyway and rub my eyes. "I'm sorry."

"No need, Mariah. You've been a great help. I know this has been difficult for you, but everything you've told us will go a long way in helping us catch the person responsible. If you'd like to come with me, I'll have someone get you home. Your vehicle is still at the victim's home, but just looking at you, I don't think you're ready to go back there right now."

I chuckle sadly as images of Justice once again flash through my mind. "I don't think I'll ever be ready to go back there. But I do need my car. The drive to my house isn't far from…" I choke on the words and look down at the latte on the table.

"I understand. Nothing about this is going to be easy." He stands. "How about we get you home?"

"I'd like that." I stand slowly. Loki follows. DJ leads me out of the room. My heart stops beating when my eyes land on her.

Lyric.

She smiles softly at me. "How are you?" She reaches out her hand and rests it on my arm. It's so warm. So smooth. The tingles I felt when she first touched me are more present than ever. I instantly get goosebumps.

I feel my cheeks heat up slightly, and I look down at my feet. "O-okay. Trying to be anyway."

"Lyric, would you be willing to give her a ride to her car?" DJ asks. "I have some paperwork to do before I get out of here."

I look up at Lyric through my lashes. Her hand is still on my arm. I can't help but wish she never lets it go. I bite my lip and silently berate myself. I don't even know if she's interested in me. She probably has men and women falling at her feet. She's so pretty with her big, hazel eyes and beautiful dark brown hair. She has the perfect figure. She's a small girl, like I am, but she has womanly curves.

26

Lyric smiles widely. "I'd love to."

"I knew you would," DJ says with a wink. He looks down at me. "Give me a call if you need anything or think of anything else, okay?"

I nod. "I will."

He smiles and gives my shoulder a squeeze before striding away. I let out a slow breath because Lyric still hasn't let go. My skin feels like it's on fire under her touch. Alive. Like everything about her makes every fiber of my being stand at attention.

"Ready to get out of here?" Lyric asks softly.

"So, so ready," I say honestly. "I just want to go home and take a bubble bath. I doubt I'll ever sleep again without being knocked out, but a bubble bath would be nice."

Lyric squeezes my arm before, unfortunately for me, letting go. "It's not something you see everyday," she almost whispers, chewing on her lip. "I'm so sorry you had to."

I give her a tired smile. "I just want whoever did this to my friend found and prosecuted. Justice..." I shake my head and hug myself. "She was the sweetest person I've ever known. She didn't deserve this." I follow Lyric out to her car with my hand tangled in Loki's fur. I don't know what I'd do without him right now. Probably fall over.

Lyric stops in front of a brand new red Camaro. My mouth drops. She smiles. "My baby. Well, one of them. I also have a wolf."

My eyes widen. "Really?"

She nods as we both get in her car. Loki climbs into the small backseat. He grumbles as he flops down. After we're buckled in, Lyric pulls out of her parking place and turns out onto the street heading towards Justice's house where my car is. The warm Florida sun is just peeking over the horizon.

"Matt, DJ, and I went to a call a few years ago. There was a breeder abusing his animals. We took the wolf pups to the shelter thinking they were wolfdogs," Lyric begins with a soft smile.

"But they weren't."

She shakes her head. "Nope. They were purebred wolves. We all decided to adopt them. We called the next day. Matt was going to take two of them, but we found out one of them had been adopted."

I smile and look back at Loki. "I saw you all bring them in. I was looking for a pet. I fell in love with Loki right away. We connected."

Lyric smiles. "We all felt connected right away to our wolves. Mine is gray. I named him Magni. Matt's is all white. He named her Tyr. And DJ's is like a perfect mix of all of them. His is white, gray, and a little brown. She's gorgeous. He named her Valkyrie. It's fitting yours is named Loki."

I reach back and pet Loki. He licks my hand. "Do ya'll have playdates with them?"

Lyric giggles. It's such a melodic sound. "We're all really close. We get together a couple of times a week. Matt and DJ have the biggest yard, so we usually get together at their house so the wolves can run."

I smile and look out the window. "It's just been Loki and me. I think he's become content knowing his family was adopted and safe." I look back at her a little shyly. "But sometimes I catch him staring listlessly at the moon."

Her eyes widen adorably. "Oh my God! You should totally bring him to DJ's house the next time we get together! I'm sure he'd love to see his family again!"

It's impossible not to like this girl. I laugh for the first time in God only knows how long at just how adorable her excitement is. But the smile quickly falls from my face when I see her pulling in behind my blue Ford Escape.

I sigh and rub my eyes. The weight of the entire night is pulling me down. I question my driving skills because I can suddenly barely keep my eyes open. But closing them isn't an option because Justice's lifeless body appears and makes my heart hurt.

"Thank you for driving me," I say softly with a weak smile as I start to open the door.

"DJ texted and said he'd like me to follow you home. Just to make sure you get there okay." She looks up at me. Her shy smile has me thinking very naughty thoughts. Like how sweet she'll taste with my tongue buried inside her when she comes.

I get out of the car, silently reprimanding myself. This is not only not the time for these kinds of thoughts, but I also shouldn't be having them about her. I still know nothing about her. She probably doesn't even like being with women. I'm not that lucky. Finding someone who makes my heart skip a beat like she does is a once in a lifetime thing. No way I am confident enough to pursue anything, though.

"It's okay," I say, though I'd love for her to follow me. Just knowing she's behind me makes me feel safe.

"Captain's orders," she says. Her smile grows brighter, and she shrugs. Her beauty is truly striking. "Can't ignore Captain's orders."

I smile. "Of course not." I wait for Loki to follow me out of her car. I take a deep breath before slowly walking to mine and getting in. I take a few moments to settle myself. Loki crawls into the back and lays down. I'm pretty sure he's as tired as I am.

I yawn and rub my eyes as I back down the driveway. I've done all I can to not look at Justice's house, but as I turn onto the street in front of her house, I take a sidelong glance at it. The tears instantaneously form.

Her eyes frozen open in fear.

Her hair matted in blood.

Her floor covered in the dark and sticky liquid.

I sniffle and reach up to wipe my eyes as I turn the corner and accelerate into the busy traffic. I glance in the rearview mirror. Lyric is following as she said she would be. Seeing her makes my heart skip a beat. While nothing about this situation is right or okay, Lyric makes things just a little bit better.

I've never gotten any of the feelings with anyone else that I do with her. The tingles. The butterflies. The heat on my skin when she touches me with her satiny hands. The goosebumps she leaves in her wake.

Lyric is such a beautiful woman. I'm not sure how to approach the feelings I have for her because I've never been in a situation where I didn't know if the person I was with was or wasn't into me. I've been with a couple of other women before, but it was easy then. We met at cocktail parties that were specifically for lesbians. Places where no one would know me. For me, it was experiential.

I smile softly and start to slow for a red light. Only my SUV doesn't respond. "What the hell?" I hit the brakes again. No response. I look down in disbelief and back up quickly. I pump the brakes again. Nothing.

The light is getting closer and closer. There are no cars in front of me, and I find myself praying for the light to turn green before I get to it. As if answering my prayers, the light turns. I fly through the intersection doing just over thirty miles an hour.

A slight hill is coming up. I hit my brakes again and again to no avail. My heart starts to race in my chest and pound in my ears. Tears sting my eyes. I hit the brakes again and again, but nothing happens. When I get to the hill, I start to speed up. The hill isn't that steep, but there's a light at the bottom.

I watch in horror as it turns yellow when I'm halfway to it. There's no way I will get lucky a second time and have it turn green by the time I get there. I look in my rearview mirror and find Lyric is watching in just as much horror as I have to be projecting all over my features. Only she's thought enough to pick up her phone. I hope to Hell she's calling for help.

I whimper. The sound brings Loki out of his slumber. He starts to sit up with a low growl. He's sensed the danger I feel. I'm approaching the light at just over forty miles an hour. It's red. Traffic is crossing.

"Loki, down!" I scream as I careen into the oncoming traffic. I whip my wheel to the right, hoping to avoid any cars with the turn into the traffic. Loki obeys and lays down.

Tears blind me.

Brakes screech.

Glass breaks.

Metal on metal crunches.

I cover my face as I hit something. Or something hits me. I'm not sure which. My only thought is protecting my head and hoping Loki will be okay. I can hear his howl as I scream. It cuts my soul.

When I finally stop, I've lost complete count on how many times I've spun.

How many times I've been hit.

I'm terrified to open my eyes, unsure if I even can. Instead, I take a moment to check myself for injuries. Pain. Numbness. Anything.

I can't hear anything. It's deathly quiet, but I don't know if it's because I've gone deaf, or if everything around me has stopped. Maybe the world has paused. Maybe the Angel of Death is coming now to take me away.

"Mariah!" someone screams. I slowly and shakily move my arms from my head. "Mariah! Oh my God!"

I groan and gingerly open my eyes. Like a fighter jet, the chaos around me slams into me. Loki is whimpering and nuzzling me. People are yelling. My windshield is shattered. There's a pole over the hood of my car. My heart jumps to my throat until I realize it's not an electrical pole. It's a street light.

"Oh God," I whisper.

"Mariah!" Lyric screams. I look slowly at her, still a little unsure how injured I am. "Mariah! Answer me!"

"I'm okay," I whisper. I clear my throat to speak louder. "I'm okay."

"Mariah, oh my God." She reaches in the broken driver's side window and grips my shoulder. Tears are rolling down her cheeks. "Matt is coming."

My brain is fuzzy. I blink a few times. "Matt... okay." I don't know who Matt is. Do I? I try to think as I shakily reach down and unbuckle my seatbelt. My hands tremble.

Lyric runs her fingers softly through my hair. I can tell she's checking for injuries. It makes me smile, though weakly. My entire body is tingly with nerves and panic at not knowing what happened.

"Just don't move, okay? Help is coming." Her soft fingertips stoke my face. Her eyes, shining with unshed tears, never leave mine. She'll never know how grateful I am for the comfort.

"What happened?" I ask quietly, watching everyone. Some are holding their heads. Some are glaring at me. Some are surveying the scene.

"I don't know... I saw your brake lights come on, but it didn't look like you were slowing down. It looked like you were speeding up. I got really scared and called Matt when you went through the first light, even though it had turned green. Then you hit the small hill and started going faster, even though your brake lights came on. I knew you were trying to slow down, but your car wasn't responding. When I saw the light at the bottom of the hill turn yellow, I knew you were going through it. I'm so glad you thought to turn, Mariah." She takes a shaky breath. "You wouldn't have made it if you hadn't."

I don't think. I turn my head slightly and kiss her palm. When she doesn't pull away, I reach up and put my hand over hers, kissing her palm again. "I'm okay..." I close my eyes and lean into her palm. "I'm okay."

As Loki rests his head on my shoulder and Lyric gently caresses my cheek, I know I'll be okay. I don't understand what happened, but I know I'll get through it.

Chapter Four

✬ Lyric ✬

I keep Mariah close to me, refusing to let her go. We're sitting on the grass. She has a blanket around her that one of the firefighters gave her after they got her out of her car. Which is smashed to hell. I don't know how she survived. I don't know how Loki survived.

Watching what happened as it was happening was heart stopping. Seeing her careen into traffic and turn the way she did made my heart drop into my toes. I can't deny her driving skills saved her life, but holy shit. I still don't know how she made it out of there. She was hit by three different vehicles. She was spun around and hit again by one of them. It sent her into the street light. She hit it so hard, it fell over the hood of her car and landed over someone else's trunk.

Matt got here while they were pulling her out. I was right by her side when they were checking her to make sure she was okay. Miraculously, she was. They didn't even advise she should go into the hospital to be checked further. They just said if she starts to feel weird, then she should go. Even Loki didn't have a scratch on him.

Matt, wearing jeans and a t-shirt and aviator sunglasses, strides over to us after talking to people and officers on the scene. I've caught a couple people glaring over here. Like what happened was Mariah being inattentive or driving drunk. I've glared right back.

Matt kneels in front of us. "You doing okay, Mariah?" he asks.

She stays huddled into herself as I rub her back. Loki doesn't move from her side. "I still don't know what happened. I just couldn't stop," she whispers.

"I saw her brake lights," I say. "She tried. Whatever happened with her brakes was intentional, Matt." I'm angry, but I try to keep my voice calm for her.

Matt nods. "I know," he says low. "I have my suspicions. Her car is being towed to our garage where our investigation team can look into it, but given what you said and what she did, I think the lines were cut."

Mariah whimpers and buries her head back into her arms. "I was afraid you were going to say that."

Matt squeezes her knee and looks at me. "Get her home. Grab some things she needs. Take her to your house. DJ and I both think she's a target now, but the department won't approve twenty-four-hour surveillance."

Mariah tenses and looks up at him with wide eyes. "What?" she squeaks.

I sigh and put my arm around her. I squeeze her gently. "It makes sense."

"Just for a couple of days, Mariah," Matt says. "Give us a couple of days to do our job and track down Justice's ex-boyfriend. We just got surveillance from the house. We have an investigator looking at it. We just need to keep you safe while we do our job. Okay?" Matt stands and holds out his hands for both of ours. He pulls us both up with ease. "Go home. Get some sleep. Both of you."

I lead Mariah to my car and help her in after Loki crawls into the back with another grumble. I don't blame him, really. It's small back there for a large wolf like him. Mariah says nothing. She just looks out the window after she buckles herself in. I let out a slow breath and pull away from the scene of the accident.

Mariah has been through two incredibly traumatic events in less than twenty-four hours. I admire her strength and resiliency. I'm shaking inside for her. If I were her, I'd be curled on the floor of the car bawling my eyes out. The fact that she isn't is something I'm starting to really like about her.

Despite the situation, I allow myself a small smile. Her lips on my palm earlier, though I know she was probably just trying to comfort me, sent jolts of awareness I've never felt from anyone through me. It was sweet. Tender. Caring. I couldn't bring myself to pull my hand away. I'm not sure I could've anyway. She was holding my hand against her cheek rather tightly. I was more than happy to give her what she needed. Especially if it meant touching her in any manner.

"So, where am I going?" I ask her quietly. I'm not sure she hears me. I'm just about to ask her again, but she rattles off her address just as quietly as I had spoken to her.

I glance at her as she shivers. The sun is high in the sky now. It's almost noon. It's warm, but I turn down the air conditioning in the car anyway. I'm sure the lack of sleep is making her heart slow a little, making her feel cold. I'm hoping it's not because she's going into shock.

She keeps her gaze focused outside and hugs herself. She leans her head against the window and closes her eyes. She doesn't move as I drive, but I take my cues from Loki that she's okay. He seems to be very in tune to her, and he's lying calmly in the backseat.

I yawn and blink sleepily as I turn onto her street. My heart immediately sinks. I'm still a couple of blocks away, but I see a lot of flashing red lights. Smoke is billowing into the sky and assaults my nostrils almost immediately.

Loki must smell it, too, because he sits up with a whine and barks. Mariah jerks. Her eyes fly open. She looks first at Loki, then me. Her eyes slowly follow ours. I hear her let out a strangled cry when her eyes fall on what we see.

"No," she whispers. Her eyes widen. The closer I get, the more tense she becomes. When I finally get to the scene, she screams. "No!"

I pull over and stop. Mariah jumps out of the car and runs towards the house that is engulfed in flames. Loki wastes no time in sprinting after her, barking. I fly out of my car and run to catch up to her.

"Mariah! Stop!"

"No!" she screams as a firefighter grabs her around the waist. She struggles against him and tries to break free. "No! No! That's my house!"

"Ma'am, you can't go in there! You have to stay back!" the firefighter pleads. I recognize him as a Captain out of our main firehall.

"I got her," I say quietly and draw her to me. She collapses in a heap. I gently lower her to the ground.

"My house!" she cries into my shoulder. Loki sits next to her and leans his weight into her. I hug her as close as I can.

"I'm sorry," I whisper into her hair as I run my fingers through it.

As I hug her, I catch sight of a piece of paper pinned to a telephone pole. I squint to make it out. Tears sting my eyes. It's an image of me and Mariah at the scene of the accident just a few hours ago. My hand is reaching through her window. She's kissing my palm. Both of our faces have big red x's over them. Scrawled in big red letters are the words 'lesbian sluts will die'."

I bite my lip and try to stay strong, but inside I'm falling apart. I know what I'm seeing. Mariah was obviously a target for someone, and I just became a target as well. I choke back the sob threatening to escape and shakily reach for my phone. I call the only person I know who will know what to do.

"Hey, Lyric. What's up? You get Mariah home?"

"Matt," I choke. "You n-need to get h-here," I whisper. "Now. Bring DJ."

"Where?" His voice is suddenly very sober.

"Mariah's."

"We're on the way. We won't be long." Matt hangs up as he's calling out to DJ. I don't know where he is. Maybe he's still at the accident. I just hope he's close.

I keep my eyes on the scene while I hug Mariah in the grass as her house burns to the ground. I keep her back to it because I don't want her to see it collapsing, which I'm sure it will do at any moment. It's nothing but a shell right now. Completely unsalvageable. Loki, though, is watching it and whining. I can't help but run my fingers through his fur in an attempt to soothe him.

I stay with her for what feels like hours to me before I see Matt and DJ pulling in behind my car. They both get out of their vehicles and make their way to us. Their eyes are on the scene behind me. When they reach us, I point to the telephone pole. They glance up. Matt pulls the picture down.

"Looks like it was printed from one of those portable printers you can hook up to your phone," DJ says quietly to Matt.

Matt looks around. "We need to get them out of here. Now."

"We'll follow them to Lyric's house. She'll need to get clothes and Magni. I'll lead. You follow," DJ says.

I look up at them both. "She's in shock. She stopped crying. Now she's just staring vacantly. I don't even know if she knows you're here."

DJ nods and kneels down in front of us. "Mariah." He turns Mariah's head towards him and forces her to look at him. "Look at me. Are you seeing me?"

She nods slowly. "My house," she whispers. "Everything was in there."

"Not important. It can be replaced," DJ says. "Right now, I know it's hard, but I need you to trust me. We need to go. Right now. I need you to stay together a little while longer."

"My house…"

"Mariah. Stop it. Look at me," DJ commands, making her jump. I watch as her eyes start to clear and focus.

She takes a breath. "DJ…"

He nods. "We need to go. I need you to go with Lyric. Can you do that for me?"

She nods slowly and looks at me. DJ helps her stand. I put an arm around her waist and help her to my car. Loki follows with his head down and tail between his legs. He jumps in the car and curls into himself in the backseat. Mariah sits and does almost the same thing.

I look up at DJ. "What are we going to do?" I whisper, closing her door.

"I need you to get some clothing for both of you. She looks to be about your size. We need to move fast. I don't want either of you out here right now. We need to get somewhere we can make a plan. Matt will follow you to your house. I'll lead you. Then we're going to our house. We'll figure it out from there."

I take a breath and nod. It's time to put on my big girl panties and be the tough girl I try to portray. I can't show that I'm falling apart right now. Mariah needs me. I need to be strong for her. We might be nothing more than strangers on our way to friends, but I already care about her more than I do for almost everyone else in my circle. Even if we're never anything more than friends, I've already decided I need her in my life.

So, as I follow DJ away from the scene with Mariah curled into herself in my passenger seat and Loki curled in a ball in my backseat, I take a deep breath to steady myself. I focus on everything that needs to be done because that is the only way we're getting through this.

First, I need to get us clothing. She lost everything in that fire. I need to grab Magni. Second, we need to get her personal items. Shampoo. Things she needs. Third, we need to get to safety. Fourth, we need a plan.

Focusing on the list going in my head will keep me from panicking. Panicking will not get us anywhere right now. I can tell by the way Mariah is rubbing her chest that she's panicking. We both can't be panicking. One of us needs to think.

"I really like you," Mariah says out of the blue.

I jolt slightly at the sudden sound of her voice and glance at her. "W-what?"

She sniffles and turns her head towards me. "I said I really like you." Her voice is as soft as her smile. "Maybe I'm off my game, but…" She trails off with a soft chuckle. "Never mind." She looks out the front windshield and focuses on DJ's black Mustang.

My heart beats so fast it causes me to take a deep breath to steady it. I can only hope she's saying what I think she is, but I don't know that I dare hope. "You mean…?"

She smiles softly again. "They say starting relationships in the midst of chaos is only asking for failure, but…" She shrugs and looks over at me shyly. "I think you're really sweet. And pretty. And every time you touch me, I feel like an electrical current is humming through my blood. I've never felt that before with anyone. I love your British accent. I love everything I've come to learn about you. Even though it's only been like a day."

I'm quiet for so long that she takes a breath and turns her head back to looking out the windshield. My heart is racing because the words that just came out of her mouth are the exact same feelings that I have. I'm so surprised that I've forgotten how to speak.

Finally, after a long while, I clear my throat. "I feel the same way," I say quietly. "I just thought it was crazy. I didn't know if you even liked women, or if you preferred men. I don't know anything about you. Just that you're strong and beautiful and sweet. Every time I touch you or you touch me, I feel like I'm on fire. No one has ever made me feel like that before. No one has ever taken my breath away before." I can feel the blush creeping from my neck and making its way to my cheeks.

"Seems a little crazy." She chuckles, keeping her attention focused on DJ's car as he turns onto my street. "Just yesterday, we were complete strangers. Now, here we are confessing our attraction to one another in the midst of a very unstable and chaotic situation."

I smile a little. "What better time than to do just that?" I pull over behind DJ and stop in front of my house. I take my keys out of the ignition and get out of my car.

Mariah follows, letting Loki out. "Is this your…" She trails off. Her mouth falls open slightly.

I furrow my brows and follow her gaze as Matt and DJ get out of their vehicles. My eyes widen. I let out a soft whimper when I see what she's looking at. All of my windows are busted out. Shattered. The outside walls are covered in graffiti. Words like 'lesbian,' 'slut,' and 'whore' are spray painted all over my house.

"What… happened…?" I ask quietly. For the millionth time, tears sting my eyes. But then I think of Magni. "Oh God! Magni!" I take off running to the house. "Magni!" I scream again.

Matt's arms snake around my waist. "We'll call out a team to take pictures and board up the windows. Right now, we need to get out of here. Whoever did this is probably watching."

"But Magni!" I yell and claw at his arm.

"Lyric. Think," he says to me. "You can't run in there half fucking cocked. Think like the cop I fucking trained you to be."

I take a breath thinking of nothing but my wolf. What if he's injured? What if whoever did this took him? What if they killed him? Despite the thoughts going through my head, I make myself calm down because Matt is right. I have to be logical. I have to go in there in cop mode. Whoever did this could still be there.

DJ is already bringing Mariah to his car and locking her and Loki in there. He gets in the driver's side and takes off. I look up at Matt completely confused. I figured he'd want to go into the house with us.

"Mariah is as much of a target as you. We need to get her out of here. Split the attention of whoever is doing this." He looks up at the house. "Do you have your backup gun?"

I let out a breath. "You know I do."

"Then let's go. We need to get in and out. Fast. Our goal is Magni. I don't give a shit about clothing. We'll buy it."

I nod and let my cop brain take the lead. This is a rescue mission. Magni is the priority. When we get to the house, I start calling for him. I don't like that he doesn't answer or come to my call or whistles.

My front door is ajar. Leading with our weapons, Matt and I quietly enter the house. It's destroyed on the inside, too. There's graffiti all over the place. There's a drawing of a giant penis in my living room. The TV is smashed. Even the refrigerator in the kitchen is tipped. Dishes are broken. My couch is torn up. Furniture is torn up and upturned.

But the priority is Magni. "Magni!" I call out, taking a chance. Matt stays behind me. His eyes continue sweeping my house.

I know him well. He's taking stock of everything. The graffiti. The windows. The furniture. Everything. Nothing gets by him. It's one of the things that makes him an incredible cop and one of the State of Florida's top trainers.

I shake my head slowly. "Why? Why would anyone do this?" I whisper.

"I don't know. Probably to scare you."

"Why not burn it down like he did Mariah's?"

"If you want my honest opinion, I'd say because he hates her. He blames her for something. My guess is she's right when she says it's Justice's ex. What he did with her is pure anger. He was trying to kill her. The fire? He was showing her he's in control. This? This is to scare you off. You're not the one he wants. At least not really. Doesn't make you less of a target, though."

"Magni!" I call once more. Finally, I hear a bark. "Thank God… He's upstairs. Probably locked in a room."

Matt nods towards the stairs. We both cautiously climb them. The wall is covered in graffiti. Pictures are shattered and ripped to shreds. When we get upstairs, I see feces outside my bedroom door and gag.

"Gross," Matt says. He reaches around me and turns the knob. The door opens with ease.

39

Magni growls viciously and barks as he charges out the door. When he sees me and Matt, though, he stops and jumps up on us. He whines and licks us both. I wrap my arms around him and bury my face in his fur.

"Oh God, Magni. Thank God."

"We gotta go," Matt says. "Let the team come in and do what they do. We need to get out of here."

I just nod and let Matt take the lead in getting us out. Magni follows, sticking close to my side. When we get outside, I barely register his words as I get in my car. Magni sits in the front seat. I pull away from the curb on autopilot with Matt following me to DJ's. Now that I know Magni is okay and Mariah is out of harm's way with DJ, my adrenaline dump has hit.

But it isn't until I pull into DJ's and Matt's garage that I let myself break down. I wrap my arms around Magni and bury my face in his fur as I cry.

Chapter Five

☆ Mariah ☆

"Mariah! Jesus Christ. I've been trying to get a hold of you for hours!" Tyler barks into the phone. "Are you okay? I got the call from your alarm company about the fire when they couldn't get a hold of you. What happened? Are you hurt? Where are you?"

I hold the phone slightly away from my ear and rub my head. When he's done hurling questions at me, I slowly put it back to my ear and curl up in the pool chair in DJ's backyard. Loki is getting to know his brother and sisters. DJ and Matt are inside making dinner. Lyric is curled up next to me watching the wolves.

"I'm okay, Ty," I say quietly. "I wasn't in the house."

"Fuck, Mariah. What the fuck happened? I've been going fucking insane with worry. My father threatened to call the Governor in Florida and send out the National Guard."

I take a breath. "Justice was… m-murd-ered." I choke on the sob and pinch the bridge of my nose as I close my eyes.

"What?" Tyler's voice portrays the shock I'm sure just lit up his face.

"She was s-supposed to come over l-ast night." I sniffle and take a deep breath. "Three hours. She hadn't shown. I went to her house. She was…" I swallow another sob. "She was on her kitchen floor. Bl-ood. Everyw-where."

"Jesus Christ, Mariah. I'm sorry."

"It gets worse," I nearly whisper. "I was at the police station answering questions." I take another deep breath. "After, one of the officers drove me back to Justice's house to get my car. I was driving back to my house. I was tired. The officer followed me. Just to make sure I got home okay. I had Loki with me. My brakes went out. The police think my brake lines were cut or punctured or something."

"Fucking hell. What the fuck?"

"When I finally got home, Lyric, the officer, drove me. The plan was that I would stay with her for a couple of days until the police figured things out. But my house…" I trail off and open my eyes. The tears stream from my eyes. Tears I didn't know I could still cry. I've cried so much, I thought I was dried out.

"So, the police think it's the same person?"

I shrug. "I honestly don't know, Tyler." I sniffle. "All they know is I'm a target. And so is Lyric."

"Lyric. The cop? What does she have to do with anything?"

"Her house was vandalized. There was a picture at my house of us together at the scene of the accident. Her hand was on my cheek. I was leaning into her. The picture and her house had all of these awful words. Like slut and lesbian and whore. The picture of us said that we were going to die. I didn't see the picture. One of the other officers told me about it."

"Jesus. Where are you, Mariah? I'm coming to get you. Now."

I let out a breath. "I'm at the police Captain's and his husband's house. His husband is a Lieutenant. He said the department won't give him authorization to put a twenty-four-hour patrol on us. He decided we'd be safer here. At least we'd be together with four wolves." I smile a little. "I found Loki's family."

"I'm happy for Loki, Mariah, but I'm not happy with this situation. I mean, as your agent, I can get you private security. But as your friend, fuck, as your family, I want you out of Gainesville until the cops figure this shit out. I'm coming to get you, Mariah."

I rub my eyes. "You don't have to, Tyler."

"I'm not arguing about this. You'll be safer here. And the cops don't have to worry about you being unprotected. You not being there will allow them to do their job. Hopefully faster."

"Tyler, I can't just leave Lyric. She's a target, too. And… I really like her," I say quietly. I know she can hear everything I'm saying, but she hasn't made any motion to move. Her pretty hazel eyes are still focused on the wolves.

"Then she comes with. Mariah, I'm not playing around. I'll be there in an hour. I was already in the sky on the company's jet when you called. Meet me at the airport." As per usual, Tyler hangs up before I can say anything else.

I hang up with a sigh. "How do you feel about New York?" I ask Lyric with a soft smile.

She looks at me with the most vulnerable eyes I've ever seen. "You'd take me with you?" she whispers.

"I would. If I'm being whisked away for my protection, you should be, too. And it would give us a chance to get to know each other."

"We need to talk to DJ and Matt," she says quietly. "If I'm being honest, though, I really don't want to be here right now. I've never been targeted like this."

"Me either." I stand and help her up. We both walk back into the house just as Matt is putting food on plates.

"I got through to my agent and friend. His name is Tyler," I say.

DJ looks over at me. "What did he say?"

"Well, when my phone was dead, the alarm company tried to contact me about the fire. When they couldn't get me, they called him. He's currently on the publishing company's jet on his way here. He wants me to go to New York while this situation is resolved." I take a breath. "Frankly, I think he's right. I think me and Lyric being here only gives whoever this is more opportunity to get to us. With both of us not here, it gives you all time to find this person."

Matt sets a plate down on the table and looks at me and Lyric, who has her head down and her hands clasped in front of her. She's standing behind me a little. Matt starts filling glasses. DJ brings the salad to the table.

"So, you're an author of some sort?" Matt asks.

I nod. "I'm a bestseller. I write romance. My publishing company is Alexander's Publishing House. It's a huge publishing company located in New York."

"I'm for getting both of you away from this," DJ says. "But I want you both to eat something first."

My stomach growls, but I know there will be food on the plane. "Tyler is going to be here in an hour. Well, at the airport."

DJ points to a chair. "Both of you. Sit. We're not going anywhere until we eat something. None of us have eaten since yesterday. And we need to."

Lyric and I both do as we're told. The chicken salad is every bit as delicious as it smells. I'm glad he made us stay because I find I'm a lot hungrier than I thought. I also don't like eating on planes. I get motion sickness. Food often makes that worse.

"So, tell us about Tyler. Where are you going to be staying when you're there? Do you have security?" Matt asks.

"We will. The publishing house will make sure of that. We'll be staying with Tyler. He has a penthouse that has a lot of security. His floor is completely private. You need special access to even get to it."

Matt nods. "Lyric? How do you feel about it?"

For the first time since we sat down, Lyric looks up. She sniffles. "I'm just worried about work and not being able to get off. I don't want to work right now. I don't think I can focus. I'd be a liability. I know Magni would be okay here."

DJ smiles. "You don't need to worry about your job, Lyric. I'll take care of it. And Magni will be just fine here. What we want to know is how you feel about going to New York with a girl you barely know."

Lyric lets out a breath. "I feel like I've known her my whole life," she says with a soft smile. She shyly looks at me for a moment before she looks back at Matt and DJ. "I think she's right. I think us not being here gives you more opportunity to find out who is doing this. I think us being here would be a distraction. I know you both. You'd be worried about both of us."

"There isn't a doubt about that," DJ says.

Matt swipes his hand down his scruffy face and looks at DJ. "They could use this as a vacation. A chance to get to know each other."

"Yeah. I agree. But I still want you both checking in. And I want security on you at all times." DJ stands and surprises me with dropping a kiss to the top of my head. I look up at him. He smiles. "I can't say I'm surprised at all that you two hit it off. I could tell immediately just by how you were looking at each other."

I can't help but laugh. "Do you know how absurd that sounds? I barely know any of you. And here I am trusting you all, feeling completely comfortable with you all, and like I've known you forever. And I'm about to run away with a woman I've known less than a day to escape someone trying to kill us both after he killed my best friend. This is all crazy."

Matt grins and DJ laughs. "Just a day in the life," Matt says.

Lyric looks at us all before she cracks up. She throws her head back and laughs so hard that her face turns red. Watching her causes me to laugh. Before I know it, Matt and DJ are both laughing. It's like all of the stress and tension we've all felt over the last day is coming out in the most insane way possible. If anyone was looking in who knew what was going on, they'd probably call the men in white coats to have us all hauled away and taken to padded rooms.

But the laughing helps. It helps to clear my mind. When we're all finished and everything is cleaned up, I'm thinking clearly for the first time since I saw Justice lying in a pool of her own blood. Leaving Gainesville during this time is a good idea. Going to New York is the best option. It's a big city. Tyler's penthouse is secure. The publishing house can get us the security we need. There are more resources and options for us there than here.

Most importantly, though, Lyric is right. DJ and Matt have a job to do. I know they are close to Lyric, but I'm also finding myself becoming comfortable with them and closer to them myself. It's not hard to do. They both are welcoming and accepting. They're easy to talk to. They're protective. It's because of that fact that I know they'd be worrying about us being here alone. They might worry with us being away, but it's unlikely we'd be followed to New York. And if we are, we'll have people with us to protect us. Tyler will make sure of that.

A little over an hour later, after three phone calls from Tyler telling me to hurry up because he's landed already, we pull into the airport. DJ drives us to the private airstrip Tyler said he was on. I get out and help Lyric as Tyler rushes towards us.

"Fuck, Mariah." He wraps his arms around me as soon as he reaches me. I feel all the tension in his body evaporate as he hugs me.

I let out a breath and breathe in the fresh scent of the only family I have as I hug him back. "I'm okay," I say into his shoulder.

"Is this Lyric?" he asks against my hair.

I close my eyes and nod. I'm more grateful than I thought I'd be that he's here. "Yes."

The next thing I know, Lyric is cuddled into my side, and we're involved in a three-way hug with one of the only people in this world that I trust with my life. The fact that Tyler didn't hesitate to pull her into his arms to join in the hug doesn't surprise me at all. It's that Lyric didn't hesitate to melt into his embrace like I had. She seems a little on the reserved side. I can't help but smile at the feel of her sinking into us with no question or tension. I want her to be comfortable with both me and the man who has become like family to me.

"We need to get them out of here," Matt says quietly next to us. "I hate letting either of them go, but we'd be crazy not to do this. Getting them out of here is priority."

Tyler looks up and meets Matt's eyes. "You must be one of the cops who helped her?"

"Lieutenant Matt Chance." Matt extends a hand. Tyler lets us go and takes his hand to shake. Matt nods to DJ. "This is Captain DJ Rens."

Tyler shakes DJ's hand. "Matt's husband?"

DJ grins. "Yep. We're also Lyric's friends. Mariah's as well. We'll keep both of their wolves with ours at our house. You take care of our girls."

Tyler laughs and nods. "Yes, sir." He looks down at both of us. "Let's get out of here. I have some arrangements to make with security. I'd like it dealt with when we touch down."

I nod because I'm too tired to do anything else. I'm not going to lie. It's nice having someone else take control. Looking at Lyric, I feel like she probably agrees. She looks just as exhausted and beat down as I feel.

Matt and DJ both hug us. Lyric clings a little to Matt for a few moments longer before letting go. Since I just did the same thing to DJ, I'm pretty sure it's because she's trying to soak up his strength.

DJ looks down at me. "I meant what I said. Call if you need anything. Even if it's just to talk."

I nod and smile softly as I look around. "We weren't followed, were we?" I hug myself. The thought that suddenly crossed my mind chills me to my core.

DJ shakes his head. "No. We weren't followed. No one knows where you're going except us."

I let out a relieved breath. "Okay. Okay, good."

"Now let's get you both on that plane and out of here so Matt and I can put an end to this shit." DJ gives me a gentle nudge towards the plane as Matt whispers something in Lyric's ear before he gently nudges her towards me.

I smile a tired smile and take her hand. I link her fingers with mine and climb the stairs that lead into the cabin of the plane. She squeezes my hand and follows. Tyler follows her. We both turn around and wave to DJ and Matt before disappearing into the plane and finding seats. Lyric scrambles into a seat next to me and immediately buckles in.

"Don't like flying?" I ask with a gentle smile.

She shakes her head. "I've been on one plane in my entire life. And it was from London to Orlando."

I buckle my seatbelt as Tyler settles into a seat across from us. He's barking orders into his phone. I watch him for a few moments until the flight attendant brings us all a cold bottle of water. I can feel the plane start to back out just as Tyler hangs up the phone.

"How did you end up here?" I ask Lyric.

"I always wanted to move to the United States. I researched pretty much my whole life on where I wanted to move. In the end, it was a small town in Texas or Gainesville. I decided the small town in Texas probably wouldn't give me the opportunities I needed to succeed. And small towns are notoriously cliquish. They don't like new people all that much. Especially someone who threatens their lifestyle. So, Gainesville is where I ended up. I've always wanted to be a cop. I walked into the department and met Matt. I started asking questions on how I could become a police officer with the department. Matt helped me a lot. He helped me navigate the immigration system and helped me with the department. The tests and everything."

I smile. "You both seem very close."

She smiles brightly. "He's my best friend, honestly. I wouldn't be where I am without him. He's helped me become who I am and accept who

I am. Really, he's helped me to love the person I've become and be comfortable with myself."

"That's amazing. That's how I…" I take a deep breath. My smile falls a little. "That's how I felt about Justice. We were both sort of navigating who we were and wanted to be. We helped each other to accept ourselves. At least, we were on the right track." I look down at my hands. "Being targeted because of who I am doesn't help."

Lyric takes my hand as the plane speeds up, getting ready for takeoff. As the plane starts rising in the air, I close my eyes and let the feeling of freedom wash over me. We're going to be okay. I know it.

Chapter Six

☆ Lyric ☆

(One Week Later)

I giggle at Mariah standing on the bow of the yacht Tyler rented to take us on a tour around New York Harbor on our way to our private tour of Ellis Island. Mariah has her hands outstretched. The wind is blowing her hair back. Her back is arched. Her eyes are closed. The water is spraying on her face. She's the most beautiful thing I've ever seen.

After a few moments, Mariah opens her eyes and jumps down. She walks back to me with a giant smile. "I'm telling you. So peaceful. I love the water. It's the one thing I miss about Duluth, Minnesota. Lake Superior is gorgeous."

I furrow my brows. "Isn't that the largest and deepest lake in the world?"

She sits next to me. "Well, the largest natural lake anyway. The deepest is in Russia. Lake Baikal, I think. Lake Superior reminds me of an inland ocean. It's so big and beautiful. And blue. When you get out away from the shore, it's just this so, so, beautiful clear blue. I'd love to show you one day." She looks at me shyly.

I blush. "I'd love to see it someday." I take her hand in mine and enjoy the view as the Captain of the yacht takes us around the harbor and closer to Ellis Island.

She smiles. "I'll take you there. It's amazing. There's a hotel right on the water that's gorgeous. It has a jacuzzi in the room, a balcony, and in the winter, it has a fireplace.

My eyes widen and I smile. "It sounds amazing!"

She takes her phone out with a happy grin and pulls up images of the hotel. As I thought, the hotel is incredible. It's beautiful. Cozy. The balcony looks out along the lake and city. And the fireplace looks incredibly inviting.

We've been in New York for a week, and everything about the city is everything I've ever dreamed. Of course, that might be because Mariah has spared no expense when it has come to seeing everything I've wanted to. Including Broadway.

We've had private security following us around everywhere we go. It makes me giggle because I feel like a celebrity, even though I'm the farthest thing from it. Mariah, though she's an incredibly popular author, doesn't attract attention here. To everyone in New York, Mariah is just another person. She's explained in smaller cities, though, she's very recognizable and usually ends up with a crowd around her. I'm happy to say Gainesville isn't like that. Mariah has as much privacy there as she does here.

Of course, that was before we ended up with a psychopath on our tail. Someone who stalks her every move. And mine as well, apparently. We still don't quite understand the entire motive. All we have is speculation. And we speculate that the killer is Justice's ex. We think he is after Mariah because of her relationship with Justice. He probably thinks they were together. We feel like he's after me because he thinks I'm with Mariah and, therefore, connected to this entire thing.

Whether that's true or not, I'm not certain we'll ever know. Matt and DJ have been checking in with us nightly. There have been no developments in the case. Only that they can't find the ex at all. He seems to have vanished. That's not at all scary. Or terrifying. I shake my head. It's a fucking nightmare and does play into our theory.

The sunshine in all of this darkness, though, is me and Mariah. Even though we both have a crazy person after us, our relationship is flourishing. We have so much in common. She writes romance novels under her pen name, Mariah Marie. I absolutely love her work.

In my spare time, I design covers. I even design covers for her, which neither of us knew. A few years ago, I was commissioned by her publishing company as their in-house designer when they saw my work for an independent author they had scouted. Now, I'm their exclusive cover designer. If I wasn't a cop, I'd make more than enough money designing covers for their authors.

I smile when the Statue of Liberty gets closer. "My God. It's so pretty."

"It's gigantic," Mariah says. She brings our linked hands up to her lips and kisses the top of my hand.

"I always thought it was gray." I tilt my head.

"Well, I suppose looking at it from a distance. Or maybe when the sun hits it just right. But it's actually made of copper and iron. Mostly. There's some steel in there, and even a little gold. But the Statue of Liberty is actually called 'The People's Statue' because it was funded by the spare change of the people of France. The stand that it's on was funded by the spare change of the American people. Because of that, the statue is mostly made of materials that the people could afford. Copper has always been considered the people's metal."

I look up at her in awe. "How do you just know that?"

She smiles. "I'm a fountain of useless facts. I research something for a book. The next thing I know, I have a ton of useless information floating around in my head waiting for some poor soul to ask me a question, so I can spew all of the useless facts."

I laugh. "Well, that wasn't really useless. I didn't know any of that."

"Truthfully, I love history. Historical facts and information are just something that sticks with me. I know things from my World History class in high school that most people probably forget by the time they are near forty like I am."

I laugh again. "I think most people forget most things from high school as soon as they leave it."

"We're just going to get docked," the Captain says. "Then we'll get you going on that private tour."

Mariah looks over her shoulder. "Thank you."

"I bet you could guide the tour yourself," I say to her.

She laughs. "I probably could."

We wait as the yacht docs. I glance back at where our security is sitting. They might look like they are relaxing in the New York sun, but I have come to know better. Their eyes are always on the swivel. They never let us out of their sight. They're always on the lookout. Always ready.

"I'm glad we came here," I say quietly. "Not that I don't feel safe with Matt and DJ, but I don't think they'd be able to be around us all the time. It's nice having security around. And us not really having a care in the world."

"It is nice. I've enjoyed exploring New York. I've been here before but never really had time to take in all the touristy stuff. I also hate big cities, but I'm learning they're nice to get lost in. No one knows who I am here. Not that many people know who I am, or care, back home." She smiles a soft smile and looks up at the statue as she stands and pulls me with her. She looks back at me, something shining in her beautiful hazel eyes that look piercing blue today. "It's been nice getting to know you, though. Away from the chaos."

I blush and look down at our linked hands as she leads me off the boat. It has been nice getting to know her on a more personal level. Most of all, I've enjoyed getting to know her expressions. When she says something she thinks might make me blush, she bites her lip and blushes herself. When she's surprised, her eyes widen, but she also gets this adorable sparkle in them. Her mouth falls open slightly. When she's deep in thought, her brows crease, and her tongue pokes out of the corner of her mouth. I've had to stop myself a few times from leaning over and licking it.

One of my favorite things, though, is when she gets shy. She can't meet my eyes no matter how hard she tries. It's not just her cheeks that blush a pretty pink, which I've learned is her favorite color. It's also her ears. But just the tops of them. She looks up through her lashes, but never quite far enough to actually see me.

Truthfully, everything about Mariah is adorable and beautiful. She's so smart. I can talk to her all night long about nothing at all. And I have. I wasn't lying when I told Matt and DJ that I felt like I've known Mariah my whole life. Now that I've been with her for the week we've been together, I feel like we're connected on a much higher level than just some idiot after us. I'm falling in love with Mariah.

✯✯✯

Hours later, after a full day at Ellis Island, Tyler pops the cork on a bottle of expensive looking champagne. I watch him with a smile. I've grown to like him almost as much as Mariah. Maybe just as much. I love that he's right here for her, for both of us, whenever we need anything.

Tyler pours some of the champagne into glasses. "To Mariah." He lifts his glass. "On another book that is sure to be a bestseller. And on my father fucking loving it."

I giggle as we both sip. My eyes widen. "Oh my God. That's so good. I didn't expect it to be that good."

Mariah laughs. "Tyler never spares any expense when it comes to wine and champagne." She gestures to the wall behind his bar. It's floor to ceiling racks of wine that, from what I'm told, are the best vintages. The rack itself is even cooled to the perfect temperature for the bottles to keep them the best they possibly can be.

Tyler looks at his phone and groans. "Fuck me. Stop texting."

I raise an eyebrow. "One-nighter go bad?" I tease.

He laughs as he sits on the couch and loosens his tie. "She's the daughter of one of my dad's business associates. My dad gave her my number. I refuse to give her the time of day."

Mariah snuggles into me on the oversized chair we've commandeered as our own. She looks at Tyler. "How come?"

He lets out a long sigh. "Because she is the definition of a socialite. Right down to the snippy and holier-than-thou attitude. My dad wants me to take her out and show her a good time while she's in New York tomorrow. I'm not doing it." He looks up apologetically. "I probably used you both for my excuse. I know I said I'd let you be alone at the World Trade Center and the memorial, but I need you."

He looks so vulnerable in that moment that my heart actually hurts for him. So, I smile. "Holier-than-thou? Let me at her. I'll kick her back down to middle-class with just my words. Just ask Matt. I've done it before

53

when a former colleague of ours tried to come between Matt and DJ to split them up."

Tyler snorts out a laugh. "I'm totally positive you'd succeed completely at taking her down a notch, but I need to hear this story now."

I giggle. "Well, the girl had a huge crush on Matt. Like…" I hold out my arms to signify how large. "Like she was totally obsessed with him. He's a really nice guy and took this selfie with her at a party we went to for the police. It was put on by the department for appreciation for their officers. This girl framed this picture and put it on her desk. She literally told everyone that they were together. Which we all knew wasn't true. Matt and DJ had been together a long time before they married. They didn't flaunt their relationship by any means, but we all knew who they belonged to, and that was to each other. So, Matt told me to ignore it."

"I get the feeling you didn't listen," Mariah says, giggling.

I shake my head with a smile. "At first, yes, I did. But then she started coming to me and saying that I needed to back off Matt. I was like, uh… girl… Matt is my best friend. You really need to back off. She upped telling everyone that she and Matt were together. I mean, explicit sex descriptions that could rival the ones you write."

"Okay, fuck. I might joke around with Mariah about my sex life, but I don't go spreading that shit to everyone in the office." Tyler shakes his head. "Come on. Have some fucking class."

"Right? No one believed her because everyone knew Matt liked guys. He has his entire life. But that didn't stop her. It was like she refused to believe that Matt is gay and was about to marry another guy. Even Matt had confronted her by that time. Hell, DJ had, too. Finally, I got sick and tired of it. She was spreading rumors and everything. I knew Matt wouldn't say it, but it was hurting him. Maybe not reputation wise because we all knew the truth and most just rolled their eyes at her, but it was hurting him. So, I marched up to her desk and told her that she would stop. I didn't give her a choice."

Mariah laughs. "Here we go. Sassy, Lyric."

I giggle. "I said she would no longer be allowed to hurt my friend. I told her that we were going to have a conversation with Chief King and she was going to be a good little girl and not say a damn word. I told her that her complete lack of respect for anyone and her delusional fantasies of a man she could never have was sickening and sad. I told her that there had to be something wrong with her head if she truly believed that Matt was or ever could be hers. And that there was definitely something wrong with her if she ever thought he could love anyone other than DJ. I grabbed her by the arm and marched her straight to the Chief's office, and told him everything that had been going on. She sat in the chair and didn't say a damn word."

Tyler cracks up, holding his stomach as he laughs. "Remind me not to piss you off."

I giggle. "So, in the end she was ordered to a psych eval. She failed. Miserably. She was fired. Last I knew, her family got her to go into a mental health rehabilitation facility." I smile. "So, if you need someone to get her off your back, I'll happily oblige!"

Mariah and Tyler both laugh. "I might take you up on that," Tyler says. "Right now, I'll be happy with crashing your date tomorrow."

I smile again. "If Mariah is happy about you date-crashing, I have no objections. Having your back when you need it is the least we can do to repay you for all your help," I say before Mariah has a chance.

She looks up at me with a shy smile and tears in the corners of her eyes. Before I have any time to process what's happening, she kisses the corner of my mouth. I can feel my cheeks turn hot as the blush hits them. I duck my head, biting my lip to hide the smile. We've done a lot of talking and hand holding. She's even hugged me. We've snuggled while watching movies. But we haven't kissed. Feeling her warm, satiny lips on mine makes me wish for more. A lot more.

Mariah nuzzles my neck and cuddles as close as she can, wrapping her arms around my waist and laying her head on my shoulder. "You know we're here for you, Ty," she says. "Even though you're a pain in my ass, you're still my best friend."

Tyler barks out a laugh. "Fuck that. I'm so much more. One day I'll get you both in bed." He teasingly wiggles his eyebrows.

I raise an eyebrow. "At the same time? Or…" I grin teasingly. "Because that might be fun."

Mariah snorts out a laugh. "Not a chance. It would seriously be like fucking my brother. Ick."

Tyler laughs. "Yeah, I'll be honest. Maybe a couple of years ago, but now it would be really fucking weird and disgusting."

I shiver. "Disturbing. It would be like me actually having a relationship with Matt or DJ." I make a gagging sound. "It would be like having sex with a family member."

Mariah giggles. "You should tell him what you told me last night that you and Matt did to DJ."

Tyler raises an eyebrow and gets more comfortable. "Fuck yes. I love hearing stories of pranks."

I smile brightly. "So, Matt and DJ have this amazing relationship where they can totally prank each other. They do it all the time. Like one day, DJ had a glitter bomb waiting for Matt when he opened his office door. It was epic. To get him back, though, Matt and I devised this totally amazing prank. I took a pic of his abs and put them on my phone as my screensaver. And he put my cleavage on his screensaver on his phone and his work computer."

Tyler's eyes widen. "He didn't!" He laughs.

I nod. "Yep. He did. And we'd flirt right in front of DJ. Openly. One day while having dinner with them, I confessed my undying love to Matt. DJ's eyes just about popped out of his head. I straddled Matt and leaned down like I was going to kiss him after telling him I wanted him and DJ more than anything in the world. Both of them. I wanted to have a threesome with them. DJ had no idea what to say. Matt looks up at me, and just before I kiss him he tells me there's a problem." I pause for dramatic effect. Mariah giggles.

"Fuck. Don't keep me waiting. What did he say?" Tyler asks.

I laugh. "He didn't say anything. I sighed as dramatically as possible and nuzzled him as lovingly as I could without laughing. Then I told him I knew. The problem was that he didn't have a pussy."

Tyler cracks up laughing again. "Jesus Christ!"

"DJ was so confused. I got off Matt's lap, and we both doubled over laughing as hard as we could. We'd had this whole thing going on for months. DJ finally figured out what was going on after that and vowed never to forgive us. Of course, he did forgive us. After calling us little fucking fuckers and throwing us both in the pool."

"Did he get you back?" Tyler asks as Mariah yawns.

I yawn and blink sleepily. "Tenfold. The prank war is never ending. We always have to watch our backs because we never know who is going to get us. I once had my squad filled with Styrofoam."

Tyler looks at his watch with a yawn as he laughs. "I didn't realize it was almost one in the morning. I'd love to hear more, but if you two intend on starting early, we should probably get to sleep."

"Mmhmm… Good idea," Mariah murmurs as she slowly gets up. She takes my hand and pulls me up with her. "I'm really excited to see the memorial." She smiles softly when Tyler leans down to kiss us both on top of the head.

"My bed is open if you want to try out that threesome thing." He gives us a teasing grin as we playfully shove him with a laugh. Mariah leads me down the hall to our bedroom.

"Ick," Mariah says with a giggle. "Penis' have cooties."

Tyler snorts out a laugh and trips over himself as he follows us. "Not once has any woman said that to me." He laughs again.

Mariah shrugs and looks up at him coyly. I can see the teasing smirk in her eyes, though. "There's a first time for everything." She bites her lip as we both look at her.

Tyler breaks first. He cracks up and pushes us both gently into the bedroom. He doesn't say a word as he laughs. Just closes the door on us. We both giggle. His warm laughter fades as he makes his way to his bedroom.

"He's really -" I let out a whimper of surprise as my eyes widen.

Mariah's lips crash to mine. She closes her eyes and tangles her fingers in my hair. She lets out the sexiest moan I have ever heard and lets her tongue tangle with mine. My knees get weak. If her arm wasn't around my waist, I'd fall.

I let my eyes close and relish in the feel of her. Her sweet vanilla and coconut lips moving against mine. Her sexy as sin breasts pressed against me. I manage to raise my own hand to tangle in her coconut infused hair. I tug gently because I can't help it. I love when she lets out another moan.

So many impure thoughts run through my head that when she slowly pulls back, I lick my lips and shiver. A quiet whimper leaves my lips. Mariah says nothing. Just smiles and leads me to the bathroom. We both get ready for bed. When I finish, Mariah is already curled up and waiting for me.

My dreams become reality when she slips her arms around me and kisses me again. The kisses are sweet. They turn so hot, though, that I feel like the panties I'm wearing are suddenly soaked and might melt off.

As if to cool me down, though, Mariah slows the kisses. We both giggle as we watch each other. Our hands explore each other's curves as we stare deeply into each other's eyes. I've never just wanted to learn every part of another person before.

Mariah smiles and runs her fingers through my hair. She kisses me deeply again. She tangles her tongue with mine and sucks lightly. Once again, I sink completely in her. Her taste. Her subtle scent. Her beauty.

She pulls away with a soft smile and snuggles me close. No words are spoken. For the first time, I don't feel like they need to be. I don't have the overwhelming desire to leave. As I close my eyes, my only thought is that I don't want this to end. I only want her.

Chapter Seven

☆ Mariah ☆

I walk slowly hand in hand with Lyric looking up at the newly built World Trade Center buildings. I smile softly, but a huge weight feels like it's sitting on my chest. Tears sting my eyes. I don't bother to hide them, though. This seems like the perfect place to let them fall freely.

The new towers look just as majestic as they do in pictures I've seen. They stand tall and sturdy. The sun reflecting off the windows makes them all look like they are made from the shiniest silver. To me, they say to the world that we are united. We are strong. You can attack us. You can think you've beat us. But you didn't. You couldn't. You never will. We will always stand tall.

"Man," Tyler whispers. "Fucking beautiful. Inspirational."

Lyric smiles. Her eyes glisten with tears. She leans into me. "It's even more inspirational in person than it is online."

"It's incredible," I say with a soft smile. "I've always wanted to see this." I take a breath. "Now that I am, it feels surreal." I squeeze her hand when she squeezes mine. I glance towards the museum. "I'm not sure I'm ready to go in there, though."

Tyler puts his hand on mine and Lyric's shoulders. "It's bound to be emotional. But we are here with each other. It would be a shame to miss out."

Lyric and I both nod. We hold each other's hand a little tighter as we all walk to the 9/11 Memorial and Museum. Stepping through the doors, though, steals all of the bravery any of us thought we had. Tyler visibly takes a breath to steady himself. Lyric sniffles and wipes her eyes. I gasp out a sad sob.

We walk through the museum wiping tears from our eyes. I don't know how it feels for them, but seeing the twisted steel, images of the devastation, and the lives lost is like ripping my soul out of my body. I feel the pain and agony. It's like everything that happened that day comes crashing back into me. Except the force is far more intense.

Crushing.

I suddenly can't breathe. I grip my chest and rub it, but I can't get enough air into my lungs. My shoulders want to tremble but don't. Nothing moves. My legs are frozen. Me. I'm frozen. It's like my connection to this place, the people, is deeper than anything I've ever imagined. I don't know why I feel the way I do.

Lyric, the beautiful soul she is, hugs me. And just like that, I'm back. I take a deep breath and close my eyes. I breathe her in. Her subtle and beautiful scent that I still can't quite figure out. Vanilla bean, maybe, with a hint of something else. I let myself sink into her. I let her center me.

"I'm sorry," I whisper into her hair.

"It's okay. This is really emotional," she whispers back. She takes my hand again as she slowly pulls back. "Tyler is looking at some pictures…"

I nod slowly and squeeze her hand. "I just got overwhelmed with emotion."

"Me too… When this happened, I got… I don't know how to explain it." She shakes her head. "Chills? Violent. I was ten. I wasn't allowed to watch the news, so I didn't know what happened right away. But I will never forget how I felt like I lost a part of me that day. It was like… painful. I've never understood why I felt so connected like that."

We walk hand in hand towards Tyler. I squeeze Lyric's hand as we join him and solemnly look at the images hanging on the wall. The voices of the ghosts from September 11, 2001, echo throughout the museum, gently reminding us all who the real heroes in the world are. Those who lost their lives. Those who fought to protect them. Those who lost their lives saving others. Those who ran into the burning and crumbling buildings while everyone was running out. Those who showed up to dig through the rubble and save as many as they could while giving the families of those who didn't make it some closure in the wake of one of the most senseless acts in world history.

I feel all of their anguish so deeply that it hurts, but I continue walking and reminiscing about where I was on that fateful day in our country. What I was doing, and how it forever changed me and so many others.

As we near the end, my eyes fall on an image. I tilt my head and step closer, feeling like I might recognize one of the men in the photo. He's covered in dust and ash. His hair and face look gray. His clothing is streaked with soot, a stark contrast to the dismal color of the rest of him.

"Huh," Tyler says next to me. He squints his eyes and crosses his arms over his chest, rocking back on his heels. "That sort of looks like one of those cops you were with back in Gainesville. The one who was a little shorter but far more broody. What was his name? DJ? Or was it Matt?" He looks down at me.

"DJ..." I trail off and tilt my head the other way. "I can't really tell. He looks younger. What do you think, Lyric?" I look over at her.

Lyric's hand has gone to cover her mouth. She makes a pained sound that I couldn't describe if I wanted to. Wounded. Tears are streaming from her eyes, but I'm not totally sure that she even knows they are falling. My heart suddenly starts racing. Lyric slumps. Her knees buckle under her, and she starts to sink to the ground.

"Lyric?" I try to catch her, but her sudden weight pulling down on my hand catches me off guard. I stumble.

"Holy fuck." Tyler catches her just before she hits the ground. He swings her into his arms. "She fainted. Grab some water or something. Meet me outside. It's cooler out there than in here."

I hurry to do as he says. I buy a water from the gift shop and run after him. When I get outside, he's got her sitting next to him on a bench and breathing deeply as he rubs her back. I slide onto the bench next to her and open the bottle, handing it to her. She takes it gratefully and sips it with her eyes closed.

After a few minutes of Tyler and I both soothingly rubbing her back, Lyric puts the cap back on her water. "My father and twin brother...," she begins just above a whisper. We both have to lean into her to hear her. She sniffles. "They took a guy's only trip." Her voice is heavy with emotion. "All I knew when I was ten-years-old was that they didn't come home. I never knew where they went for their trip. My mother never told me. My family said they disappeared. They were never found." She takes a deep breath. "I just found out they lied to me... They would have been notified. At least my mother would have."

I look at Tyler, slightly confused. "Did... you see something we didn't?"

She nods and swallows. Hard. "That was DJ in that picture," she whispers. "He once told me that his Army unit was dispatched to help..." She looks up as she pauses. She takes another pained breath and gestures around the site of the memorial. "Here."

Tyler takes a breath and lets it out slowly. "The other people in that picture."

Lyric nods. I quickly understand and whimper. The pain she feels is suddenly so evident because I feel it, too. I feel the insurmountable sadness because it's what she feels. The connection I've felt with her since I first met her feels cemented and stronger in this moment than it had at any other moment in the last week.

I sniffle. "DJ pulled your dad and brother from the rubble...," I trail off on a whisper.

Lyric looks down at the ground and nods slowly, almost imperceptibly. "I doubt he knew that, but yes... The people he was kneeling over and looking down on were my dad and twin brother. I remember after their divorce, my dad wanted to make sure that Luca and I were handling it okay. He'd planned on taking me somewhere after. I remember he told me that. I didn't know they came here. Luca never really felt the same connection to America as I did, but my mum had to have known. She kept it from me... I don't know why she'd do that."

Tyler and I both hug her tighter. "Maybe to protect you," he says.

Lyric shrugs. "Maybe. But knowing her? It was more denial. My mum is schizophrenic and paranoid. She lets the voices take control when she doesn't want to deal with something. I'm sure they made up a story to her, and she believed it because she didn't want to believe they were dead.

Although, to me, thinking they were missing and not knowing what happened is far worse."

I kiss her shoulder and wrap my arms around her comfortingly. I press my lips against her neck. "I don't know if it's any comfort, but at least you know now what happened."

She nods and takes a hard, shuddering breath. She sniffles and stands a little shakily. "I want to take a picture and send it to DJ," she says quietly.

Tyler and I both stand to help her. We each take a hand and walk with her back inside the museum. Tyler leads us back to the picture with DJ in his military uniform kneeling over the two people in front of him lying on the stretchers on the ground. Lyric whimpers as she trembles. But she takes the picture she wanted and sends it to our friend.

"Excuse me, miss," a quiet female voice says from behind us. We all turn towards her. She's a petite woman dressed very professionally in a simple black skirt and t-shirt that says 9/11 Memorial and Museum. "I don't mean to bother you, but I saw your reaction to this photograph. I was just wondering if you'd be willing to tell me the significance of it to you. I'm the head of this museum. This photograph has always been a bit of a mystery to us." She looks over Lyric's shoulder and frowns. "We've never been able to identify the military man to thank him for helping us get these individuals home."

Lyric sniffles and turns to me. She wraps her arms around me and bursts into tears. I hug her as tightly as I can, tangling my fingers in her hair and swaying gently with her. I look up at Tyler, pleading with him to take the lead.

Tyler rubs up and down Lyric's back as I hug her. He clears his throat and looks down at the woman. "The military man is a friend of hers. He's a Captain with the Gainesville Police Department in Florida. The two others that he's kneeling over are... her twin brother and her father. Until today, she never knew what happened to them. Her mother never told her. She thought they had gone missing on vacation and were never found."

"Oh my goodness." The woman puts her hand to her heart. "I'm so sorry to hear that." She puts her hand on Lyric's shoulder. "I have information on these two. If you'd like, I'd be happy to make you a copy."

Lyric looks up at her slowly with teary, wide eyes. "Really?" she asks quietly, her voice laced with hope and desperation.

The woman's eyes shine with unshed tears. She nods and pulls out a card. "If you'd like to come back here before you leave the memorial today, I'll have everything gathered for you. My name is Kate. If you could have your friend contact me, I'd really be interested in speaking to him. He was responsible for saving several lives with his diligence in digging through the rubble. He also helped to find several others who didn't make it but were at least able to give their families some closure. Your friend stayed here for over a month helping us. We were never able to identify him, though."

"I'm sure he didn't want to be," Lyric says quietly. I feel her body, though tense, swell with a sense of pride for DJ. "Captain Rens doesn't view himself as a hero. He's retired from the military now, but he's the best Captain anyone could ask for. And an even better friend." Lyric bravely wipes her eyes.

I'm overwhelmed with such admiration for the woman standing in front of me. Admiration and something else. Something stronger. Love? Is it too soon to feel that way about her? As I watch her shift into the warrior Queen she is, though, I know. I really do love her.

The thought makes me smile. I take her hand in mine once more and kiss it, not giving a single fuck who sees or what they think of a woman kissing another woman's hand. I know the stigma that comes with being who I am. I've lived with it my entire life.

We lead Lyric back outside. I gently squeeze her hand and run my thumb comfortingly over the top of her hand as we walk towards the place where the previous towers stood. They have been turned into a beautiful fountain of cascading water. The names of every single person who lost their lives that day are etched into bronze around the fountain.

"I wonder where their names are," she says quietly.

"Well, we have all day long," I say with a soft smile. I tuck her hair behind her ear because I can't resist my innate need to touch her. "We'll find them."

Lyric jumps a little when her ringtone sounds. We stop at the beginning of the North Tower memorial while she answers it. "DJ," she sniffles and puts the phone on speaker so we all can hear.

"Lyric. Fuck, honey. I didn't know," he says, emotion cracking his voice. "I didn't know. When I saw your text after seeing the picture, my heart fucking broke. I didn't know that was your dad and brother. If I had known, I'd have told you long ago when you told me they were missing and had never been found."

"It's okay." She swallows around the sob forming as she wraps an arm around her waist. I wrap mine around her and rub my hand up and down her arm. "Mariah said at least I know now. It's hard and really sad, but she's right. At least I know. It gives me a small sense of closure. I don't know what happened. I don't know how they were caught there, but the woman who manages the museum said she has information for me and will make a copy for me."

There's a pause on the other line. I hear a deep voice murmuring in the background. Matt. I'm glad he's there with DJ. Finally, DJ takes a breath. "They were the first people I'd come across in the search. We were all told to wait. The building was unstable. But our commander overruled the commander on the ground with the FDNY. He said there were people trapped. If we waited for the building to stabilize, there wouldn't be anyone to save. So, we mobilized. We went slow, like we were in the battlefield and doing all we could to keep our feet off IEDs or any type of explosive. But the goal was to get people the fuck out."

"I understand," Lyric says quietly.

"I came across them buried in the rubble from the North Tower. Tower one. At first, they were talking. They weren't far down. Maybe seven feet. Me and a few others started digging them out. We pushed debris aside. When we got them out, they were alive, but in bad shape." DJ pauses when Lyric whimpers and sniffles. The tears have started to fall again. "Do you want me to stop?" he asks softly.

She shakes her head. "I want to know... I need to."

DJ takes a breath and sniffles himself. "Your dad begged me to help his son. I didn't know their names. I didn't need to. I just knew your brother needed help. His breathing was ragged. I'm sure from all the smoke he'd inhaled. We yelled for medics to get over there with oxygen for him, but they couldn't get to us. The debris was starting to shift. It was weakened from the fires burning around us. They were still putting out hot spots. So, I carried him out. My partners carried out your father. I didn't get far when..." He pauses again. Lyric leans against me until I'm taking almost her whole weight. "When I had to start breathing for your brother. I was giving him air as I was trying to get them to safety. He still had a heartbeat. But he never woke up. I never got him back. I'm sorry, Lyric."

Lyric sniffles. "You tried. You tried, DJ. I know you. You tried as hard as you could."

There's another long pause. DJ takes another breath. "By the time we got him to a safe area, the medics were waiting. They took over CPR. They tried to get him back, but it just didn't happen. Your dad was breathing, but it was labored. Hard for him." DJ swallows. "I never knew what he meant, but as they were working on him, he took my hand and your brother's. He asked me to tell his family he tried to protect his boy. That part I got, though I had a feeling I'd never be able to pass on that message. I knew we were losing him, so I said I would. Then he said something that has haunted me for years."

I shiver at his tone. "What was it?" I whisper.

"Make sure my daughter knows this wasn't her fault. Don't let her live with the grief. She'll blame herself. And her mother will let her. Make sure she knows we love her and will always be watching her. Guiding her." DJ takes a deep breath as his voice cracks. "Just after that picture was taken, I'd written a note with his words on it. I told the team in charge of the de-" He cuts himself off on a sob. It makes Lyric tremble and cry into my shoulder as she clutches her phone.

Tyler gently takes it from her hand. "You told the people in charge to make sure his family gets the note," Tyler finishes for him.

DJ sniffles. I know he's composing himself. DJ is the strong one. The one who is always the brick wall for everyone else to lean on. He's never the one to fall. Never the one to break. DJ is the one who helps everyone else back to their feet. He's the one who puts them back together.

After a few moments, he lets out a breath. "Yeah. I'm sorry, Lyric. I wish I'd known. I wish I'd taken the invitation to tell my story when my unit got a letter from the director of the memorial. All she knew was that my unit had been there. We didn't sign in with our individual names. We signed in as a unit. My commander told me he'd gotten the letter. He said the other guys were going to tell their stories, but I declined. I didn't want to be viewed as anything more than a man who was there to help. I knew they'd view us as heroes. That's not what we were. It was never what it was. I knew that your dad's and your brother's belongings and... them... I knew they'd all gotten home safely. That's all I cared about."

"I n-never saw the l-letter," Lyric whimpers. "I n-never knew they'd g-gotten home."

DJ sighs. "I guess I was afraid of that. But I held out hope and thought if I needed to intervene, I'd get some kind of a sign." He pauses for a couple of moments again. "There's one more thing."

"W-what?" Lyric cries as I hug her and gently sway with her. I'm amazed we haven't attracted a crowd. People throw sympathetic looks our way. Some wipe their eyes. But no one has stopped to gawk. I thank all the Gods for that.

"He… wanted me to have something. The chain… around his neck. Your brother was wearing a similar one."

Lyric's hand flies to her throat. I look at the silver chain she's gripping and cover my mouth. "Oh God," I whisper.

She lets out a sob. "A sh-ship. With a wave be-hind i-it."

"His ship was -"

"Yellow-g-gold," she finishes. "Luca's w-was red. Mine is…" She trails off.

"Purple," DJ whispers. "The wave in the background is yellow-gold, red, and purple."

"He was going to take us on a cruise…" She closes her eyes and grips the necklace in her fist. "We wa-wanted to go to the Norwegian Fjords. J-just us."

Tyler and I lead Lyric to a bench as she talks to DJ. I don't think she could stand anymore if she tried. She needs to decompress and regroup. Bond with the one person in the world who knows what happened to her dad and brother and will be honest with her about it.

As I rub her thigh and leave gentle, soothing kisses on her neck, I make myself a promise. I will take Lyric on a cruise one day when she's ready. To a place where she can bond once more with her dad and brother.

A place called the Norwegian Fjords.

Chapter Eight

✯ Lyric ✯

DJ and I talk for almost an hour. When I hang up, Mariah is still sitting with me on the bench while Tyler grabs us drinks and a hotdog from a nearby vendor. I sit quietly. Mariah runs her fingers through my hair, letting me process everything that's happened today. I mentioned to her that my brother and father had gone on a holiday and never returned. I've always thought I could use DJ or Matt or department resources to try and find them or find out what happened to them, but I was never brave enough to ask or do it on my own. I didn't expect this. None of us did.

Tyler sits down next to us and hands out the drinks and food. "I remember my dad worked in Tower One when it all went down. He had just started his publishing firm. The plane hit a few floors above his offices. I was in school when the word started spreading. I was just starting my first year of college. I ran out of class and immediately came here. They wouldn't let me through. By the time I got here, the towers had come down. It was chaos. I couldn't get through to my dad on the phone. My mom was freaking out. She was calling me every minute."

I swallow a bite of the hotdog, suddenly famished. "I'm sure she was worried." I take a drink of the cool soda.

"We both were. Fuck, my whole family was. I kept telling the people blocking the area off that I'd help look for survivors. I had to find my dad. It wasn't until hours later when it was dark that I finally got a call from my mom. He'd made it home. But by that time, they were looking for volunteers to help with water and getting the survivors home. Or at least helping them call home. I was already there. So, I started helping those who needed a hug, food, water, a phone. Anything. I didn't go home that night. I didn't go home for a week. I slept with the firefighters and the police when they laid on the sidewalk to sleep for an hour or two. It was a stark contrast to the life I lived. I never wanted for anything. Many said I was born with a golden spoon. I probably was." He chuckles and looks down at his hotdog. "That day changed my life. It changed a lot of lives."

"That was very noble of you," Mariah says softly.

Tyler shrugs. "I felt like it was my duty as a person. When I finally did go home, it was only to sleep. I hugged my family a lot because I'd seen a lot of death in that week. But I kept going back. I went back every single day for months. I took a year off school after it was over because I had to clear my head. Get right with myself again. I almost joined the military because I wanted to kick the asses of those that fucked with us and almost killed my dad. My dad, though, told me that, while he wasn't telling me not to do it, make sure that it was what I wanted. I went backpacking in Europe with a couple of my friends. When we came back, they joined the Marines. I went back to school and went to work for my dad as soon as I graduated." He looks up at the memorial. "I never came here. When it was finished being built. I didn't come for any of the ceremonies. My parents did. Even my friends. But not me."

"How come?" I ask, tilting my head after finishing my lunch.

He looks at her with a pained smile. "For a long time afterwards, I'd had nightmares. The people we pulled out who didn't make it… Well, they screamed at me to save them. Every time I closed my eyes, I would see the face of someone we couldn't save that day. Sometimes, they still haunt me. It took me years of therapy to get to the point where the guilt didn't eat me alive. After a while, I just became numb to it. I played my role well. But at night, I was a whole different person. I drank. Partied. Fucked around with a lot of women. I did drugs. Actually, it was Mariah that brought me out of it. She was my last chance, according to my dad."

I look at Mariah with wide eyes. "I didn't know that."

She blushes. "I didn't either. Not right away. After I was signed, I moved here for a little while until I figured out where I wanted to go. It was just a couple of months during the transition from moving and starting my own life as an author and doing what I wanted. And it was only because I didn't have anywhere else to go. Tyler told me I could live with him. He took me out to a few of those parties. And I told him that I didn't want to work with him. I told him I was going to his father to demand the best like I was promised. He obviously wasn't. He was the best at one thing."

Tyler grins. "Being a mess. She told me I was the best at being a mess. And she was right. I woke up one morning to her bags packed. She said she found an apartment. I asked her where. It was in a really bad part of town. Nightly shootings. I told her no. She told me I wasn't her boss. I told her no, but I was her friend and her agent. My fucking job was to protect her and her interests. But she didn't listen. She walked out. I was hungover as fuck. There was a naked woman in my bed with cocaine residue on her stomach. I was wearing nothing but boxers stained with vomit. But all I could think about was her living in an apartment next to a gang member and ending up shot. I ran after her. She was already out the door and down in the lobby by the time I got a grip. I looked fucking crazy. I looked like shit. But I didn't care."

"That was the day he turned his life around." Mariah smiles as she finishes her lunch. "A lot of people would enter rehab or something for drug and alcohol addiction. Not Tyler."

I look back at Tyler, engrossed in the story. "What did you do?"

He shrugs. "Stopped. Cold turkey. I stopped going to parties. I ordered the woman in my bed a cab. I quit the drugs. I stopped drinking. I still drink wine or champagne, but I know my limits and don't cross them. I don't drink when I'm out, unless it's a glass of wine or champagne at dinner. I still pick up women, but in different places that are more classy, and I'm always sober."

I stare at him in amazement. "I'm truly just honored to know you. Your success story is inspiring. I don't see that often as a cop. I usually end up at the same houses dealing with the same idiots over and over again even after they've gone and graduated from drug programs or alcohol programs."

He smiles. "Thank you. But I really owe it to your girlfriend. I don't think I'd be here if not for her."

I blush and duck my head when he calls Mariah my girlfriend. I glance shyly at her. She's beaming. Her beautiful hazel eyes are sparkling a piercing blue. My heart skips a beat because I know what I'm seeing is everything I feel.

Love.

I'm in love with her. After only a week, I'm ass over head for Mariah. I can't envision my life without her. I can feel the shift between us. The bond we already started to form feels like it's strengthened exponentially. My mouth goes dry. I want to lean in and kiss her perfectly full lips, but I stop myself because I'm not sure we're there yet.

When she leans into me and takes the kiss I wanted to give her, I have no more doubts. No more fears of her possibly not feeling the same way. As we sit on the bench in the middle of the 9/11 Memorial kissing, my heart fills with a type of love I have never in my life felt for another human being. It's pure. Unconditional. It's hope.

She slowly pulls away, and I instantly miss the silky feel of her lips on mine. The gentle yet slightly demanding pressure. Her tongue lightly flicking against mine. I let myself fall into the depths of her eyes. Her smile warms my soul.

It's Tyler's whistle that breaks my gaze from hers. "Now that was sexy as fuck," he teases. Mariah laughs and swats his shoulder.

I elbow him with a giggle. "Gross. I'm starting to think of you like she does."

He looks at us both in mock horror and groans. "Not the brother zone. It's worse than the friend zone. Pretty soon, I'm going to start looking at you both like family and all of my fantasies will be fucking gross."

Mariah and I both crack up as he stands shaking his head, but we can both see the teasing smile playing on his lips. Mariah stands and tugs me with her. We both follow Tyler to the memorial, hand in hand. DJ said my family was found in Tower One. We start looking at each and every single name in silence. Mariah keeps a hold of my hand the whole time. We stick close to Tyler, as he leads us.

After a few minutes, he stops. "Hey, I think I found them."

I look up hopefully and a little scared. "Really?" I squeeze Mariah's hand. My heart starts to pound.

He nods. "I think so. Come look." He takes a step to the side so Mariah and I can look. He leans over and points.

My lip trembles. "You found them," I whisper over the lump in my throat. I trace their names as I say them. "Luca Sharpe." I sniffle. "He never got to live. He was so young…" I swallow the lump in my throat. Mariah rubs my back and hugs me. "Benson Sharpe…" I smile softly and quietly laugh. "He wanted to call me Brensa." I wrinkle my nose at the name and laugh a little louder. "It was his nickname for me. He said I was his little girl and should be named as such. Luca always rolled his eyes and said that I'm his twin. My name should start with the same letter as his."

Mariah and Tyler laugh quietly with me. Mariah kisses my cheek. "It's a pretty concoction of his name," Mariah says with a teasing grin and giggle.

"We can call you Brensa," Tyler says with a wink.

I can't stop the laughter that bubbles up and escapes through my tears. I wipe my eyes. "Sometimes, I hear that name when I'm alone. It's a little insane, but that's how I know my dad is still with me. And then I can hear Luca laughing, and him rolling his eyes becomes so prevalent in my mind's eye that I know he's with me, too."

"That's not insane, babe," Mariah says with a soft smile. "They'll always be with you in your heart. And I believe they are always watching over you. So, when you hear them laughing or hear them saying something, I really feel like it's them just saying hello."

Tyler smiles. "I couldn't agree more. Sometimes, I think I hear my grandmother's laughter or smell fresh baked chocolate chip cookies when I'm alone at home. I think it's her way of saying she's still looking out for me."

My soft smile gets brighter. "Thank you both for this." I take out my phone and snap a picture of their names. "This day has been emotional but incredible."

"Why don't you lean down like you're hugging their names? I'll take a picture," Tyler says as he gently takes my phone.

"Okay." I smile and lean down like I'm hugging their names. Them. "I love you both," I whisper. "So much." I close my eyes. "I'm so happy I found you both. That I know what happened. I feel… more whole." On a whim, I turn and kiss their names. I'm sure the copper is probably horribly dirty, but I feel like I need to do it. Like my heart is being pulled to. I sniffle. "I know you're still with me. I'll see you again one day. I'm glad you both are safe and together up there. I hope I'm making you proud."

I stay like that with my eyes closed for several moments. With each passing second, I feel more and more healed. The water cascading over the walls of the memorial is a soothing and incredibly peaceful sound that calms my heart and soul. I'm relieved that I know what happened to them now. I hate the way they were taken from me, but I am happy that DJ was with them. I'm happy they are together. And I know they are still with me. I've known it since that fateful day back in 2001.

I kiss my fingers as I stand back up and place them over their names before taking a step back into Mariah's waiting arms. Tyler shows the pictures he took. I blush at how many are on the phone, but my favorite is the one he caught of me kissing their names. My heart feels so full of love for them that it physically hurts me. But I'm so happy I know what happened to them that the pain of losing them so horrifically is forgotten. At least for now.

Right now, I'm just satisfied. They didn't abandon me as I had thought so many times over the years. I know they wouldn't do that to me. I know they loved me and would have come back if they could have. But some crazy part of me thought maybe they left to get away from my mother. Maybe they didn't want me to be with them.

I kiss Mariah's shoulder as we continue our walk through the memorial. "Where were you when the towers fell?" I ask quietly.

She smiles softly and looks down as we walk. "Uh. I was in school. My dad is bi-polar and paranoid delusional. He pulled me out of high school my freshman year. It was just after the Columbine Massacre."

I furrow my brows. "Columbine?"

She nods as we slowly walk. "Mmhmm. It was a school shooting at a high school. The two kids who did it had been planning it for a long time. They went to the school with homemade pipe bombs and guns." She shudders. I shudder with her and hold her hand tighter. "They killed a lot of people. Then they killed themselves. It was the deadliest school shooting in United States history for many years. Until…" She tilts her head. "Sandy Hook, I believe. Since then, mass shootings seem to just be getting more and more common." She shakes her head.

"People are becoming more and more desensitized to it, too. That's the worst part," Tyler says.

"Anyway." Mariah lets out a breath. Her thumb rubs absent circles over the top of my hand, sending goosebumps up my arm. "My dad thought that on the anniversary of Columbine, my school was going to have a school shooting. Instead of pulling me out for a day, or even a week, he pulled me out for the rest of the year. He said he'd homeschool me, but didn't. He allowed me to go back the next year, though. I was totally caught up by the middle of my Junior year. I would have been able to graduate with my class. But he pulled me out again."

"What the hell?" I ask, shaking my head. "Why?"

"Well, he said it was because of the mass shootings. There was a shooting scare in Billings, Montana, according to him, the same time as Columbine. Nothing came of it, but he said it happened on Hitler's birthday. And then the next year, my Sophomore year, there was apparently one in Butte on Hitler's birthday. Nothing came of that either, but my dad had concocted this whole thing in his head that Billings was the largest high school. Butte was the second. Bozeman, my school, was the third. So, there was going to be a school shooting at my school that year. And again, instead of pulling me out for the day or week, he pulled me out my whole year."

"And that fucked up the fact that you'd just gotten caught up," Tyler finishes for her.

She nods with a sad smile. "I couldn't graduate with my class anymore, even if he'd allowed me to go back. I begged and pleaded with him to let me do summer school. I could have still started my senior year with my class. He didn't. And we ended up moving to a much smaller city where the high school, middle school, and elementary school were all connected. The city was established as a city, but the population was like four hundred and three people. And we didn't even live in the city. We lived in a bus remodeled to be a living area. There was a kitchen, a couple of beds, a bathroom, and a small sitting area. And then there was an edition built off of that that had three bedrooms, a living room, and a sitting area."

My eyes widen. "That couldn't be up to code…"

"Nope. Not even close. It was three miles out of town. I had like four neighbors who lived on the road I lived on. My only friend was a mile up the road. But all of that aside, my dad said I could go back to school and finish. I told him to fuck off. I was tired of getting pulled out. I had decided that I'd get my GED or something when I turned eighteen. Anyway, a little while after that, I begged my mother to come get me. My dad had slapped me across the face hard when I was late coming back from my friend's house one night. I had fallen on my way home. I twisted my ankle pretty bad, but I knew he'd be upset. I got up and hobbled my way the last half mile home. I was late by maybe five minutes or so. He screamed and yelled at me. He slapped me so hard, I saw stars. And he didn't even care about my ankle, which was about the size of a baseball by that time."

I sniffle and bite my lip. I kiss her arm and squeeze her hand. "That's awful."

She nods. "It was. I was having a really hard time anyway. I was depressed. I had severe anxiety. Depression. PTSD from being molested as a kid. He didn't care at all. No one did. I walked into my room. I wrapped up my ankle and sat on the floor with my headphones in listening to the Backstreet Boys. I didn't really realize what I was doing, but I had totally zoned out. When I came to, I was staring at a picture of my grandmother with a knife to my wrist. I didn't cut myself, but I had been close. I stopped because of her. Instead of slitting my wrist, I got up and called my mom. I told her to please come and get me and bring me home, or I was going to kill myself. She didn't say anything more than that it would take her a couple of weeks, but she'd be there. A week after I turned eighteen, my mom drove from Minnesota to Montana and took me home."

"Oh, Mariah…" I whimper and hold her hand even tighter. I'm pretty sure I'm close to breaking it.

"It's okay, beautiful girl," she says.

I blush. "No one has ever called me beautiful…"

She kisses my cheek. "You are."

I blush darker. "Thank you."

"So, after I moved back to Minnesota, my mom enrolled me back into school. I graduated two years late, but it was okay. New place. New people. People who had no idea who I was or why I was graduating at nineteen instead of seventeen. September eleventh happened at the start of my Senior year."

"Glad you weren't with your dad when that happened," Tyler says.

"You aren't kidding." Mariah chuckles. "I was in my first period class when things started happening. I didn't know anything, but when I came out of class, my friend, Nate, was waiting for me. It wasn't unusual. He was always waiting for me after class. We liked walking together. But as soon as I looked at him, I knew something was wrong. He asked me if I'd heard what happened. I hadn't. He told me that two planes hit the towers in New York, and they were saying it might be terrorists. We walked to our next class together, but the teacher wouldn't put it on TV. We went to our third class. The teacher wouldn't put it on for us. I don't know about Nate's, but he met me after class, and we walked to our Study Hall together. The halls were totally silent. It was honestly really eerie. A high school. No one was saying a word. The only sound was locker doors closing."

"I can imagine." I watch Mariah wide-eyed.

She nods. "It was a big school. Three floors. Lots of students. To walk down the halls with hundreds of other kids and have no one saying a word is creepy. When we got to the room our Study Hall was in, the teacher had it on the big screen. It was live. It showed the towers coming down. It showed the damage. We were all in shock. No one said a word. Nate and I just sat there hugging each other. About half way through, my boyfriend showed up. He was a cop. He said my mom had sent him to get my brother and me. She wanted us home because there were rumors about an attack on our harbor in Duluth. That we were going to be next. Disable our harbor, disable the nation's shipping. Not all of it, of course, but Duluth's harbor is a huge part of the nation's shipping. The world's, to be honest."

"That's so scary." I rub my thumb soothingly over the top of her hand as she had for me minutes ago.

"It gets even more scary. I was pretty numb seeing everything. They were calling it worse than Pearl Harbor. They said it was the next Pearl Harbor. And things like the worst attack on America ever. But what scared me the most is that my boyfriend wasn't just a cop. He was also a Captain in the Air National Guard." She takes a deep breath and guides me to a bench. She sits and pulls me next to her. I snuggle into her. Tyler sits on her other side.

"Did he get orders to go to New York?" Tyler asks quietly.

Mariah shakes her head. "No. He was ordered up into the sky to patrol the harbor. They wanted him to fly. All commercial flights had been grounded. The only planes allowed up were from the military. He was under orders to shoot down any other planes still in the sky who weren't communicating with Air Traffic Control. That would mean shooting down a plane that could have civilians on it. My heart hurt for him. It hurt for the people on the planes that crashed. It hurt for any other people who were still on commercial planes in the sky. There were a lot of rumors going around that there were several missing planes. There was some kind of intelligence that suggested a plane was flying to Duluth. It was complete chaos. He was being ordered to duty immediately. He was barely able to hug me and let me know what was going on before he had to leave. And my brother didn't want to leave school. So, I was alone watching the towers come down over and over again. I was crying, screaming, crying more."

"You were alone." I lay my head on her shoulder and play with her fingers.

"I was. I ended up going for a walk. A friend, who was also a cop, saw me and said I needed to get to the gas station and help if I could because it was mayhem. I worked at a gas station not too far from my house at the time. So, I said okay. I thought it would be a good distraction. But it wasn't. Everyone who came in thought the gas prices were going to go up to over five dollars. The credit card machine crashed. We ran out of gas. I ended up directing traffic with the police department. People would pump gas and move and park off to the side so others could get to the pump to pump gas. But they hadn't paid first, so we thought we had drive-offs. We had to have two squads blocking off each exit. They couldn't leave without a receipt. We had people coming over the bridge from Wisconsin to our gas station because it was just off the bridge and twenty cents cheaper. Traffic was backed up onto the bridge."

"Sounds like chaos," I whisper.

"By the time my boyfriend picked me up, It was well after midnight. I was in tears and shaking. I was so worried about him having to shoot down a commercial plane and the potential of getting attacked. I knew shooting down a commercial plane would break him because he'd be killing innocent people. There are laws of war. Killing civilians is a war crime. But that is what he was ordered by the Government to do. I thought we were about to go into World War III. By that time, I was just starting to be able to control my anxiety. It went off the charts that night. My boyfriend spent the entire night holding me, and most of the next day. I almost ended up in the hospital. The only thing that kept me going was him. That he'd been released from duty for at least a little while. But everyone who was off during the night was ordered to be on call."

"That's so awful." I wrap my arms around her.

After a few moments, Tyler chuckles. "Sounds like we all have our stories of that. Just as painful in some ways as everyone else."

Mariah and I both nod as we sit holding each other. Tyler finally joins in and wraps an arm around us both. With a gentle New York breeze blowing through the trees above us, I feel more connected in a way with everyone who died that day. Everyone who helped clean up the wreckage. Those who helped save lives. Tyler. DJ.

But mostly, I feel more connected to Mariah. The deep love I'm starting to feel for her is unlike anything I've ever felt before. I can't imagine my life without her in it. I don't want to. I just want to be with her for the rest of our lives.

Chapter Nine

☆ *Mariah* ☆

"It was a hard day," I say quietly into the phone while I yawn. I shiver and pull the blanket tighter around myself as I look out at the city lights from the balcony of mine and Lyric's room. "Lyric fell asleep an hour ago."

DJ yawns. "And you couldn't sleep."

I look at the time on my phone and shake my head. "I'm sorry. I didn't realize it was almost two in the morning."

"Don't worry about it, Rih."

I curl up in the chair and yawn again. I called DJ because I can't seem to quiet my mind. Over the past week, DJ has become one of my favorite people to talk to. I feel really close to him. I may not like everything happening, but I am glad I met him. I'm glad I met Matt. I'm beyond grateful for meeting Lyric. People sometimes never meet their person. I didn't think I was destined to. But fate always has a plan. Even if I don't understand it.

"I guess I've just been thinking about everything. I'm wondering how things are going there. I love being here with Lyric and Tyler, but I want to come home. I miss Loki and you guys. And I know Lyric misses

Magni and you guys. Every time she hangs up after talking to Matt or you, she looks so sad."

He chuckles. "Lyric hates big cities. They make her feel like she's dead. Loki. Come here, boy." There's a little shuffling. "Good boy. Lyric is not a big city girl. She's good for a week or two, but after that, she starts to feel like her soul is getting sucked out of her."

"I know the feeling."

"Here. Maybe this will make you feel better." There's a little more shuffling before I hear a low rumble.

My eyes widen. I smile. My spirit honestly feels like it's lifting. "Loki!" I exclaim. I still stay quiet, though, not wanting to wake Lyric. He rumbles a little more before I hear what can only be described as a loving whine and soft nuzzle. "Aww... I miss you, too, boy. So much." I sniffle. "I love you, Loki. I hope I'll be home soon." He growls a little.

DJ chuckles. "I think that was him saying he misses you and doesn't like that I sent you away. He doesn't like me very much right now. He quite intentionally ignores me, but if Matt talks to him, he'll do whatever he says."

I can't help the giggle that bubbles up and escapes my lips. "He must blame you for me not being around."

"Yeah, that was the first time he actually came when I called. But I think it was because I was holding up the phone, and your face was on it. He misses you."

I sniffle a little. "I miss him, too. I miss home. I don't know where I'm going to go when we get home since my house no longer exists. But I miss Gainesville. I miss the small-town feel. New York is just so... big."

"Well, we're trying. I promise. We know through Justice's video footage that we recovered that her ex is the one who killed her. It's right there in living color. We know he's the one who burned down your house thanks to your neighbor across the street and her Ring system. That's also a huge fucking break. And we know through Lyric's security system that he's the one who broke into her house. So, we know who we're looking for. The real problem is that Richard McAdams doesn't exist."

I slump because I knew all of this. DJ and Matt told Lyric and I all of this a few days ago. "What about the law office he said he worked at?"

"He doesn't. We showed the picture we have of him and everything from Justice's security footage. They've never seen him. No one who works in that office has."

I rub my chest and sigh. "Are they lying?"

"Maybe. But we have a squad out there. They haven't seen him either. Coming or going from the building. We also got the employee roster. No one works there by the name Richard McAdams. Matt and I both think that name is an alias."

I shake my head slowly and furrow my brows. "How is that possible? They were dating for a while. Wouldn't she have picked up on that? I mean, I guess we sort of suspected a few things he was saying to her were lies. Like the law office. But we didn't really think he was lying about his name. Not for that long."

"I don't like saying I don't know, honey, but I really don't. All I can tell you with any kind of certainty is that Matt and I are both on this. Hell, the whole fucking department is on it."

"I just wish there were developments."

"Rih, the only development you need to worry about is developing your relationship with Lyric. Matt and I will take care of everything back here. We'll find him. We might not have a real name, but we'll find him. I have his license plate. It's registered to a company I've never heard of. We're tracking it down, but I think it's fake."

"So, another dead end." I sniffle. "I'm starting to feel like we're going to be in New York forever."

DJ chuckles. "Rih, just give us a little time. We have a lot to go on, and we are working on it. Diligently. You and Lyric need to be strong for us. Enjoy the vacation and each other. Let me and Matt deal with the shit going on here. I just sent you a picture of Loki. He's piled into a wolf pile with his siblings. He misses you, but he's happy to be reunited with them."

I smile. "Great. I've lost my wolf."

DJ laughs. "Nah. But you'll have to let him visit often."

"I'll probably end up living with you until I find my own place again anyway."

"I told you, Rih. Matt and I don't mind. We already moved Lyric's stuff over here and put the stuff she doesn't need in storage. She doesn't feel safe there anymore. Kind of sucks, considering how much she used to think of\ her home as her safe haven. But she's selling it now after what happened. The neighbors across the street from us are selling soon anyway. Their house would be ideal for you and Lyric."

I chuckle and look over at Lyric on the bed. "She looks so peaceful."

"It's been an exhausting day."

I watch her for a few moments before standing. "I don't think we're ready to move in together. We just kissed for the first time today."

"You two are meant to be together. We saw it when you first laid eyes on each other. Take it slow if you want, but you need to tell her how you feel. Lyric will wait until she knows how you feel before she says anything. She's a hell of a cop and will take the lead when she needs to in the field, but at home? It's a whole other story. That girl is very shy and hesitant. Submissive even."

"So am I."

"I can see that. But nowhere near her level. I can see you coming out and taking the lead before she ever would. You two are good for each other, Rih. Just… trust me when I say that you need to tell her how you feel. She won't be the first to say it."

I smile softly. "Okay. I trust you." I yawn. "Thank you for waking up at two in the morning to talk to me. I didn't want to wake up Tyler or Lyric. We've all had a hard day. The memorial took a very emotional toll."

"Yeah. It did on me, too. I cried for a little bit in my office earlier. But I'm okay. I called that woman and gave her my story. I sent her an email detailing everything. I couldn't fall asleep myself, so I was just down in the gym working out."

"My day wasn't as tumultuous as theirs… I mean, I was alone and worrying about the man I was in love with at the time. Or thought I was. We'd never done more than kiss and cuddle and talk. We just realized we'd be better friends. But that didn't mean I didn't care deeply for him. It was hard knowing he was in the air and might have to shoot down a civilian aircraft." I sigh. "Duluth was on edge because of the ports. We had no idea if more aircrafts were in the air. Where they were coming from."

"I remember the military was put on alert. The Air Force was patrolling the skies all over the country, but I remember Duluth being a huge concern. Bombing the ports would cripple the shipping industry for a little while since it's such a busy port, and so much international product goes through it."

"It was scary. But not what Lyric or Tyler experienced. Lyric lost her family that day, even though she didn't know it. Tyler spent a long time helping clean up and pull people out. He didn't go home for a week. It sent him into a huge spiral with drugs, alcohol, and women."

"It was a difficult time for everyone, honey. We all had our own experiences. All you can do now is get some sleep. Cuddle with Lyric."

I smile at my sleeping girlfriend. I bite my lip at the word. I've never used it before, but I want it so much with her. I say goodbye to DJ and drop the blanket I had wrapped around me on the chair in the bedroom. I crawl in next to Lyric. I try not to wake her, but I feel her stir. I curl in close to her and run my fingers soothingly through her hair.

"Brr..." She shivers. "You're cold..." She blinks sleepily up at me.

"Sorry. I was outside... I couldn't sleep, so I called DJ and talked to Loki a little."

Lyric smiles softly and snuggles her head against my chest tucking it under my chin. "I really miss them and Magni. I love being here with you, but I want to go home. I miss everything." She traces shapes over my shirt on the side of my breast.

I inhale sharply but quietly. I haven't been touched by anyone but myself for a long time. It feels good, but mostly because it's her. I close my eyes and kiss her head. I tighten my grip on her and run a fingertip up and down her arm, leaving a trail of goosebumps in my wake. I really like that I have that effect on her.

"I know. I want to go home, too. DJ said just give them time. He knows we miss home."

"I know how police work goes, so I don't mean to sound like a brat, but I really wish they'd hurry up." She chuckles quietly.

"I know." I lick my lower lip and smile when she shivers under my touch. I trail my hand down to the side of her breast and do what she's doing to me. I trace shapes. I'm sure she's doing it absently. I'm not. She's driving me crazy.

I feel her turn her face slightly. Her lips are close to the mounds of my breasts. I feel her lips caress them, sending tingles throughout my entire being. I shiver, but not because I'm cold. Lyric's fingers are making their way down my side. She grips my hip and looks up at me. The

83

completely innocent look in her eyes tells me that she really has no idea what she just did to me.

I smile. I'm about to show her. I slowly prop myself up on my elbow and let my hand make its way back up her body. We both wear tight tank tops and panties to bed so I know my hand is doing what I'm meaning it to. It's sending heat through her as she'd done to me. I tangle my fingers in her hair and lean forward. I capture her lips in a kiss meant to make her toes curl.

She moans and lets out a whimper that makes my clit throb. I'm wet for her. I can feel it. A delicious sensation I haven't gotten for anyone but her fills my entire soul. Warm. Comforted. Yet so hot that I want to jump her.

But not yet.

Right now, I just want her tongue in my mouth. I want my tongue tangling with hers. I let out a moan of my own and suck lightly on her lower lip before plunging my tongue back into her mouth like I'm fucking it. Lyric makes me lose complete control, and I let the feeling wash over me until I feel like if I don't pull back, we'll both suffocate.

I had gotten so lost in her sweet taste and sexy moans, I didn't realize her hand had moved to my tits. Under my shirt. She gently squeezes my nipples and tugs them lightly as she kneads my breasts. My eyes widen slightly when she tugs me down to her lips. As I had done with her, her tongue finds mine and tangos with it. She nips and sucks on it, scraping her teeth along my lower lip and moaning softly.

I let my hand fall to her hips and push her shirt up. Pulling away from her kiss, I give into the need, the desire, to bury my face between her supple breasts. I run my tongue along her nipples, taking my time with each. Lyric arches into me and tangles her fingers in my hair.

She tastes as sweet as she smells. A hint of something exotic. At least to me. Vanilla bean. I lavish her soft skin and hardened pebbles because I can't get enough. She tugs my hair a little but pushes me closer as she moans. Her breathing is heavy. Her chest heaves with desire and need.

With the hand not gripping her hip for dear life, I reach up and play with the nipple I'm not sucking on. With my thumb, I gently scrape the other hardened peak at the same time I use my teeth to softly bite her. She lets out the most adorable squeak.

But before either of us can take it too far, I pull back with a smile and kiss up to her neck. I wrap her in my arms and hug her again. She's breathless and lets out a content sigh. I love that I made her feel that way.

"Where did that come from?" she whispers into my chest shyly.

I smile and run my fingers through her soft, silky hair. "You're just beautiful and irresistible. And I'm so proud to call you mine."

"Mmm... You are beautiful, too," she murmurs. "And all mine."

Finally calm enough to relax, I let my eyes fall closed and allow Lyric's steady breathing soothe me into sleep.

Chapter Ten

☆ Lyric ☆

(Two Weeks Later)

"I've always wanted to visit Las Vegas," I say with a smile.

Mariah tightens her grip on my hand as we walk down the strip, our security close to us. "Me, too. I've never been here. I was supposed to come a couple of years ago, but it didn't end up working out. I was doing a book tour for my series' completion. That was the one you did special edition covers for. I was handing them out at the events to the first hundred people who showed."

My eyes widen. "I loved those covers. That was for your dark mafia series, right?"

She nods and smiles wider. "Mmhmm. Everyone loved those covers. I swear. I should have come out with them and did something else for the limited edition." She laughs.

I giggle. "I may have outdone myself on those ones."

"Damn right you did." She tugs me closer and turns to kiss me. I love the feel of her lips against mine.

I'm instantly soaked for her, but I force myself to pull away. We're in the middle of a busy part of Vegas. No need to embarrass either of us. "I really wish our room was ready."

Mariah's eyes catch fire. "Maybe it is now."

I giggle as she tugs me towards the MGM Grand. The hotel couldn't be more perfect. It's the location of the convention, but also the hotel I've dreamed of staying in. The giant golden lion out front is gorgeous. For it being in the center of the strip, the rooms are surprisingly quiet, or so the front desk person told us. I suppose it wouldn't matter much anyway since Alexander Publishing House got Mariah a penthouse suite to stay in for the duration of the convention. It has a private elevator to the floor we are on, which is good for security.

We walk into the lobby. I'm in just as much awe as I was when we walked in here the first time. It's modern. Gorgeous. Pristine. Everything I've dreamed it would be. I don't even care that I probably look like the biggest tourist.

I smile giddily and take out my phone when it rings. I smile even wider when I see who it is. "Matt! It's amazing here! Did you get here? Where are you? Are you here?"

"Well, we did just arrive, but there's this chick in front of us who is bouncing like she's going to pop right off Earth and head right for space. Damn good thing the woman holding her hand is keeping her on the ground."

I furrow my brows and look around the lobby in search of whoever this woman is who is more excited than me. It's not possible. "Where?"

"She's wearing a purple tank top and short as fuck shorts."

I squeak. "She is not wearing what I am! Well, minus the short shorts." I look down. "Okay, maybe they are a little short. But it's really hot!"

"Well, I don't know what you're wearing, but the girl next to her is wearing shorts even shorter than hers. Practically show her ass cheeks. And the pink tank is tight. Shows off all the curves she has and more."

I narrow my eyes as I catch on. "You asshole. You see me and Mariah."

Matt cracks up. "Is that who I see?"

I turn towards the door and see DJ bent over holding his sides and Matt grinning like the asshole he is. "I hate you." I hang up with a teasing pout.

He grins and waves. "Hey, girls!"

Mariah laughs as we both bounce-walk over to them. I throw my arms around Matt. She throws hers around DJ. Then we switch. Matt and DJ are here for their anniversary. They've been planning it all year. It's lucky it ended up being the same weekend as this convention. Mariah was booked for it at the last minute. Considering how cooped up we've been over the past couple of weeks since the 9/11 Memorial tour, this convention is an amazing reprieve.

"Oh!" Mariah says as she takes out her phone. "I know you guys said you have a room and it's fine, but Tyler upgraded your room to one of the penthouses. He said it's next to ours."

DJ shakes his head with a chuckle. "You didn't need to."

"I know. But Tyler has ways. And Lyric and I wanted to do something nice for you for your anniversary. So, the penthouse is part of it. The other thing is the helicopter tour of Hoover Dam. I know Matt really wanted to do that."

Matt smiles. "I did. But I sacrificed it for the actual ground tour for DJ."

"Well." Mariah shrugs. "Now you get both. And an awesome penthouse, courtesy of Alexander Publishing House."

DJ laughs. "Hell, I'll take it. I saw pictures of the penthouses while we were booking our room. I almost reserved one, but they were booked."

I giggle, knowing the strings Tyler pulled to get them the suite. "Now, you have one."

"But if anyone asks, you're part of Mariah Marie's security team," Tyler says, coming up to us with his nose in his phone. He hands us all keycards to our room. He's in full agent mode. It's fun seeing the switch from Mariah's best friend to her badass agent. "Both suites are ready. Take the private elevator up. It says penthouse. You can't access it without a special card, which will also open your rooms. If you need me, I'll be grabbing the schedule for your speech tomorrow night and setting up the booth for this weekend. We need to market your new book." He looks at his watch. "Dinner for the five of us and your two security guards at seven.

Meet at Crush." He walks off towards wherever they are holding the convention without glancing up at any of us.

"Well, that was a little intimidating," DJ says, staring after him. "He just dictates everything without looking up?"

I crack up. "DJ, seriously? You do that. Tyler is literally a younger, less hot version of you."

DJ grins. "You think I'm hot?" He winks. "Sorry, sweetheart. I'm taken," he drawls, exaggerating his Texas accent and putting his arm around Matt, pulling him close to his side.

Mariah laughs. "So is she." She tugs me possessively to her side. I know she's teasing, but it still makes me blush. "You'll have to fight me for her."

Matt laughs. "I don't think we would want to fight you. If you're anything like your girl, you probably fight fucking dirty. I happen to like my dick. And DJ's, too." He wiggles his eyebrows, causing us all to laugh.

"What do you say to going upstairs?" I ask quietly, suddenly very shy at how close I am to Mariah and very aware of how tightly she's holding me. Her thumb is lightly stroking my hip. I feel like shockwaves are being sent straight to my clit.

"Yes," Mariah says, looking at me with a shy blush. But I can see the heat in my eyes reflected in hers. We haven't done anything more than makeout, but I want more. So, so much more. I'm hoping that look means she does, too, because her touch is driving me to pandemonium.

Matt and DJ lead us to the elevator for the penthouse level. I stand shyly holding Mariah's hand. My heart is fluttering in my chest. Butterflies are searching for pretty flowers in my stomach. I have never in my life been so nervous and excited to be with anyone. Everything feels different with her than it has with anyone else.

I glance at Matt and DJ. I'm so close to them, but I don't want them to see the effect Mariah is having on me right now. Lucky for me, I don't think they are paying either of us any attention. The way they're gazing into each other's eyes and holding each other's hands makes me believe they don't even know there's anyone else in this elevator.

The thought makes me quietly giggle. Mariah glances at me curiously but says nothing. When the elevator doors open, she tugs me ahead of DJ, who is forced to take a step back. My eyes widen at her, but the fact that she's just as excited as I am to take this step makes my entire world erupt in flames.

Matt laughs as they follow us out into the hall. "Have fun, you two!"

I blush a furious shade of red, nearly running after Mariah's sudden speed walk. I don't get a chance to look back at Matt and shoot him a glare or smile or anything because I'm afraid I'll trip over my own feet.

But that doesn't stop me from making a smart remark. "As if you ain't gonna be bent over for DJ within seconds of closing the door! Try not to be loud. I don't need to hear my brothers fucking."

DJ cracks up. "The girl ain't wrong. Try not to scream my name too loudly."

Matt laughs. "Well, now I'll be fucking sure to!"

Mariah opens the door as I giggle. She pulls me inside the suite, pausing only to take it all in as the door closes. "My God in Heaven," she whispers.

My mouth drops open. The floor to ceiling window spans the entire sitting room and shows off the best of the Las Vegas strip. The plush couch and oversized chair are pure white and look so soft, I want to sink into the cushions and never come out. There's even a small kitchenette and bar.

I blink a few times. "Holy…"

Mariah shakes her head like she's coming out of a daze. "It's so pretty."

"And super quiet." At that exact moment, I hear Matt scream out something explicit. I blink at the wall then at Mariah. "Or not."

Mariah laughs. "You realize he's probably going to make as much noise as possible now. I know how competitive you all are."

I giggle. "You're probably right." I give her a shy smile. "I can't let him win."

She gives me a wicked smile. "Then we should probably get started with all of those fantasies I've had running through my mind."

I blush as I run behind her while she tugs me into the bedroom off the sitting room in the suite. "Fantasies?"

"So many." She turns to me. "Like how I'm positive you taste sweeter than anything I've ever tasted. And even sweeter when you're screaming my name."

90

My eyes widen, and I let out a soft squeak. "This is a very different Mariah." I blush darker and look at her through my lashes. "I like her. She's a little naughty."

"You ain't seen nothing yet." She pulls me to her and kisses me so deeply, my toes curl.

"Holy fuck, DJ!" Matt yells loud enough for us to hear. We both look at the wall behind the bed in our room incredulously.

Mariah looks at me and blinks in confusion. "Is their bedroom on the other side of the wall from ours?"

"Um…" Something crashes to the ground, and I jump slightly. I look at Mariah. "We cannot allow them to win this game." My competitive spirit soars to the surface. Suddenly, it's not just about how much I want Mariah's tongue between my thighs. It's about besting the men I consider my family.

Mariah shakes her head. "Nope. We will be winning." She tugs me to her again and kisses me until I'm moaning and dizzy.

Before I'm aware of how it happened, Mariah has me on the bed and is straddling me. Her fingers are entwined with mine, and she's holding my hands above my head. Her tongue is doing things to my mouth that make me wet and wishing it was deep in my pussy instead of tongue fucking my mouth.

Mariah moves her hips against mine. The friction I need where I need it, though, is withheld. Mariah's hands are all over me, but not where I'm silently begging her to be. It's been so long, and while I'm shy as hell, I'm overcome with a maddening want no one else has ever caused. Only her.

Her hands explore my body as she kisses me, but it's not enough. It will never be enough. DJ is fucking Matt so hard in the next room that the headboard of the bed is pounding against the wall with each of his thrusts. Not that I am or ever would be attracted to them, but knowing that Matt is getting everything he needs makes me want Mariah so much more.

"Oh, God…," I whisper and plea as I arch into her, silently begging her to do something more with me then just touch or kiss me.

Not that I'm complaining. Mariah's mouth sets my entire body alight, but I want, no, need. I need more. If I don't get it, I'm going to die. I'm sure of it. I'm going to die of the torture of my pleasure being denied.

Mariah nips my neck as she sits up on her knees, still straddling me. She pulls me up to her by my wrists and tugs off my shirt and hers. She reaches around and releases me from the confinement of my bra and catches one of my nipples in her mouth while she grips my other breast.

My head falls back, and I moan. "Holy, shit... yes..." Finally. Oh, God, finally. I reach around her and remove her bra tossing it, not caring where it lands.

I love Mariah's tits. They're large, and I've allowed myself to get lost in them several times during our heavy makeout sessions. I love that when I nip her nipples or pinch them, she jerks into me and nearly screams. I do the exact same thing for her. Neither of us have ever done it for another person. It's something that shocked us both when we told each other.

In search of driving her to the same level of madness she brought me to, I grip both of her tits and tug her nipples. She moans against my nipple. The vibration sends shockwaves directly to my already soaked center.

Her fingers find the button on my jean shorts. She pushes me down and tugs the shorts down my legs. I don't like wearing panties, so when she sees I'm completely bare for her, her mouth drops open slightly.

"My God, you're so pretty," she whispers while she very obviously lets her eyes trail over my body.

My whole being erupts with goosebumps. I'm fairly certain the blush in my cheeks has found its way down my body. I fight every urge I have to cover myself under the scrutiny of her penetrating gaze, but I refuse. I want her to see me. Touch me. I want her to lick me. I want whatever she'll give me.

"Fucking hell, DJ!" Matt yells again.

I arch into Mariah when her tongue finds my nipple. I moan and reach above my head. I giggle and bang the headboard against the wall, but the giggle dies on my lips. My eyes roll back in my head when I feel her kissing down my body and teasing my clit with the featherlight touch of her fingernail. My hips jerk up.

"Oh...," I moan. I keep pushing the headboard against the wall, but it's haphazardly. Mariah's tongue is making a tantalizing trail down my body. She circles my belly button with it and nips. I jerk. The headboard slams against the wall. "Fuck!"

Mariah giggles and kisses the rest of the way down to where I want her the most. She looks up at me. "I've wanted this for longer than I think is appropriate."

I'm trembling for her. I lick my dry lips and nod. "Me, too. Mariah, I feel like I might explode. Please…"

She grins. A devilish glint lights up her eyes. She slowly spreads my pussy and licks my clit just one time. It's so light, but my clit is throbbing for her. It's so sensitive that she could blow on it, and it might make me come.

"Oh my, you are soaked, aren't you?"

"Mariah, I'm not above begging. I've wanted this for what feels like a literal eternity." I tug her hair and pull her towards me. "Fuck…" I moan when she finally gives me what I want.

Her tongue laps from my pussy to my clit and back again. She's slow and deliciously languid as she chases my release. I'd buck into her, but she's managed to somehow grip my hips. She holds me down as she tortures me with her licks. She nips and sucks up to my clit and back down to my pussy.

I can feel myself getting wetter and wetter. I'm careening so close to the peak of my pleasure, speech is near impossible. I can already tell my release is going to be insanely beautiful. Mystical. Something I've never experienced before in my life. Not that I haven't orgasmed. But I'm near blacking out. No one but her has brought me to this point.

My pussy clenches around her tongue as soon as she dips it inside my wetness. She thrusts hard a few times. My fingers grip her hair tighter as I tremble and shiver, riding her tongue. When she replaces her tongue with two fingers, I swear I lose consciousness for a moment. The pleasure starting to rip through me is so intense that I can't hear anything but my heart thundering in my ears.

"Mmm… yummy. Come for me, baby. Please let me taste you," she whispers.

"Mariah!" I scream as my release washes over me. I wouldn't be able to stop it or control it if my life depended on it. I'm sent flying over the edge with such violence that every spasm of my pussy makes me arch off the bed and slam the headboard I'm now holding onto for dear life. "Fuck! Mariah! I'm coming! It's coming!"

"Holy fuck, DJ!" Matt screams as something hits the wall hard enough to make our bed shake.

I jump, startled, just starting to come down. The howl-like scream coming from next door makes my eyes widen as I stare down at Mariah in pure shock and utter amusement. Mariah smiles as she licks me clean.

When she's finished, she settles herself on her knees and looks at the wall. "Hey, you guys! You might end up coming through the wall next time!" she yells as she laughs.

"Round one goes to us!" DJ yells back.

I slap my hand over my mouth as I snort out a laugh. "Holy God."

Mariah smiles. "I can't even deny them that win. But they are not winning round two. I swear to God I'll make you scream the whole time."

I shake my head. "My turn."

It's Mariah's turn to blush. Unlike my clothes hastily being removed, I push her back against the bed. I kiss from her neck and breathe against her skin. I trail my tongue over her mounds as I worship her curves featherlight with my fingertips. I nip her nipples one at a time and suck as I lick each one in turn over the very thin lace of her hot pink bra.

"Oh… Lyric," she breathes. She arches into my mouth. I leave bumps along her smooth skin in the wake of my touch. Her reaction to me makes me wet all over again.

I kiss down her stomach, scraping my teeth along her skin as I make my way down to where I know she wants me. "I can smell your arousal. I never thought I'd say those words." I look up at her. She's turned a furious shade of a yet to be named color. "So beautiful. And you smell divine."

"Lyric." Her hands fly to her cheeks. "No one has ever said that to me before."

I shake my head. "I never have said that before. But it's so different with you."

"Jesus mother of fuck! Matt!" DJ yells. We can hear the bed moving again.

"My God! Did you switch? How are you old men handling this?" I yell through the wall. Matt is only forty. DJ is fifty. I'm only thirty, though, so calling them old is one of my favorite things to tease them about. I really don't think they're old at all. Yet, anyway. I giggle to myself.

They both crack up. "Shut up and fuck your girl, you brat!" Matt yells back.

"Holy fuck!" DJ yells. Something crashes to the ground in their room.

"Don't mind if I do!" I call back, giggling as I turn my attention back to my girl.

Mariah laughs. "This is going to be a long night."

"I'm up for it if you are." I shrug with a wicked gleam in my eye as I lean down. I undo the button on her sexy short shorts I've been dreaming of taking off ever since she put them on. I give into my dirty fantasies and take them off with my teeth.

I scrape her skin lightly with my fingernails after throwing her shorts and panties. I lick and kiss up her thighs. She starts panting and squirming, but I'm zeroed in on her center. The beautiful prize I've been wanting to taste ever since I laid eyes on her.

I slide one finger inside her. She clamps down on me. I'm so surprised, I nearly forget what I'm doing and look up at her. She lets her eyes close and her head fall back. Her body arches slightly as her pussy pulses for me.

"I... didn't expect you to be so tight," I whisper, curiously.

"I haven't... been with anyone for a while..." She pushes herself up on her elbows and looks down at me. I thrust slowly. She moans as she watches. "I don't use toys. Just a bullet."

I bite my lip in anticipation of what's about to come. "Be ready to scream," I say as seductively as I can, even though I'm dead serious. The pants and moans coming from the next room are sending my competitive spirit to a whole other level. But being between Mariah's thighs is sending it even higher. I want her to scream for me. I want her to scream my name. It's something I've never cared about until now.

Mariah watches as I slide another finger as deeply and slowly as I can into her pussy. I moan when she does and start thrusting. I flick my tongue across her clit. Her head falls back again. Her pussy clenches. She jerks into me.

"Oh!" She grasps the sheets underneath her. I take her clit into my mouth. "Ah! Lyric!" she screams.

I suck on her beautifully sensitive bud as I swirl my tongue around it. I thrust my fingers slow but hard and as deeply as I can. I spread them and twist them. I feel her tighten even more. I know she's about to come.

"Not yet," I plead. "Don't come yet."

She trembles. "Okay," she moans as I suck her into my mouth again.

I have plans. I slide my tongue from her clit to her pussy. Just as she's starting to protest against my plea to not let her come, I replace my tongue with the thumb of my other hand. I continue to thrust my fingers, quickening my pace only slightly. I slide my tongue in with my fingers and start a tortuous tongue fucking while I thrust my fingers inside her. I rub her clit at the same pace I'm thrusting.

"Mmm…," I moan. "So good." The vibration from my voice has the desired effect on her.

"Lyric! Fuck, yes!" she screams. "Ah!" She thrusts her hips with my fingers. I feel her pussy start to spasm erratically. I'm not sure how much longer I can get her to hold out before she loses control as I had.

I thrust faster and faster starting to crook my fingers inside her as I lick and suck. I alternate between flicking her clit back and forth and rubbing it. Her thighs tremble. Her hands grasp at anything she can grip. She grabs her tits, still blinded inside her bra. She pushes them together, causing them to spill out of the tops even more than they already are.

She writhes and thrashes. Her feet and legs spread wider before trying to clench around me. I'd hold them so she can't close them, but I'm too busy pushing her off that ledge she'd made me career off of just a few minutes ago.

"Lyric! Holy shit! I'm gonna come. It's coming! I'm coming!" She throws her head from side to side as she arches and thrusts her pussy against me. "Fuck! Yes!"

"Fuck, Mariah. Come for me. I can't wait to taste you."

"Ah!" She arches off the bed and squeezes the comforter under us in her hands. "Ah!" she screams again. "Lyric! Fuck, yes!"

"Oh, fuck yes, Matt!" DJ yells just after Mariah.

Her orgasm hits her, and she comes so hard that she squirts. My eyes widen as I eagerly lap all she gives me up while I slow my licks and thrusts, helping her to come down. She pants and writhes. Her pussy collapses around me. When she finally stops coming, she's breathing hard.

I crawl off the bed with a giggle. Mariah watches me curiously with only one eye open and continues taking deep breaths. The just fucked look all over her is beautiful, but there's one thing that is slightly more important to me right now then staring at the girl laying naked in bed who is all mine.

I put my hands against the wall next to the bed and press myself against it with a huge smile. I slap the wall as hard as I can. "Guess what, Matty? I just made my girl squirt!"

Mariah giggles as I crawl over and into bed. I kiss her deeply as I lay next to her. Matt and DJ are both silent for such a long time, I start to think that maybe they escaped the room before I made my declaration.

Mariah sighs as she looks at the clock. "We should probably get dressed. If we aren't at dinner when Tyler says, he'll go all hotshot agent on us and drag us downstairs kicking and screaming."

I can't help the giggle. "I am pretty hungry after that. I won't need dessert, though." I lick my lips.

She giggles and playfully swats my arm. "You tasted pretty sweet, too, you know."

I blush and hide in her neck.

Just as we're getting up, I hear a slap against the wall. "Round two goes to you," Matt says. "No fucking way I could top those screams. We'll call it a draw."

Mariah and I both laugh as we head to the bathroom to clean up. As we dress, I watch Mariah both shyly and in complete awe. I never really believed I'd find my person. I'm a complicated individual. I like being submissive. It's who I am and something I've recently come to accept. But I enjoy a little control as long as I know what I'm doing is right.

With Mariah, she gave me all the signals that everything I was doing was pleasurable. She didn't make me tell her to come or command her, even though I did. I'm not comfortable with commands unless it's something that feels right. With us, it's natural and instinctive.

I'm never letting this go. Never letting her go.

Ever.

Chapter Eleven

☆ Mariah ☆

I look at the faces in the crowd of people. No one would know I'm gripping the podium I'm standing behind so tightly, my palms are probably bleeding. I do not like people. I don't like speeches. I don't like so many eyes on me. The anxiety I work so fucking hard to hide from the world is difficult to hide. I'm fighting tooth and nail to not flee. It doesn't help me in the slightest that I have a target on my back, and no one knows where the fucker is.

But I'd never deny the aspiring authors in this audience, who have come to see my presentation, from getting the knowledge they seek. I've been them. I know how hard it is to navigate through this world. Traditional publishing or self-publishing is not easy. So much shit goes into it that it becomes a full-time job. People could go bankrupt if they don't do it right. If I can teach from my experience, I'll do it.

I also love my readers. They are the only reason I do book signings. I know without them, there would be no me. I'd still be writing, but I'd be struggling. This is my passion. Corporate America is not, and never has been, what I wanted for myself. I didn't leave the job willingly, which not many know, but it was the best thing that ever happened to me.

My anxiety took control. I couldn't keep up with my metrics. I couldn't even force myself into the office, but working at home didn't work either. I fought off the thoughts of being a failure who would never succeed at anything and did my best to get myself out of the dangerous hole I'd fallen into. I clawed and worked my way back up only to be fired. I spent a few months depressed as hell and fighting thoughts on how I wasn't ever going to be good enough. Then I said fuck it and started focusing on what I wanted to. I quit the corporate world and never went back.

This. Writing. This is what I need to be doing with my life.

"So, as you can see," I begin after a short pause as people look over the screen behind me. "There are a lot of advantages to self-publishing, but you have to be wary of the costs and not fall into the trap of endless advertising. Spending a grand every single month and only making just over a grand in sales is not worth it." I grip the podium even tighter as I swallow hard. "It will take time for you to make your money back on all of the other things you'll be dropping funds into unless your book just takes off. Unfortunately, the reality is that doesn't often happen, no matter how good your marketing strategy is. How good your book is. It happens. I'm not saying it doesn't, but it's rare. Getting into this business takes blood, sweat, and tears. That never ends. How many of you have heard of *Courting Obsession*?" I look out over the hundreds of people filling the room. Most are shaking their heads, but a few raise their hands. I choose one near the middle of the room. A guy. "You. In the middle. Red shirt."

He stands as someone gives him a microphone. "Hey. Brian. Thanks for calling me. *Courting Obsession* is one of your earlier works. It's been unpublished now. I'm hoping you'll tell us why because it's a good book."

I give him a soft smile as he hands the microphone back to the staff member and takes his seat once more. "Well, Brian. I'm happy to tell you." I take a deep breath. My palms are starting to hurt. I force myself to release my grip on the podium. At least a little bit. "*Courting Obsession* was one of my earlier works. I worked super hard, just like all of you, to get the book, and my name, out there. Truthfully, I had no idea what I was doing. I took a lot of hits and stumbled quite a bit, but I managed to get it published on my own. I formatted it on my own. I edited it by myself. I had a cover created by someone I paid quite a bit of money to. I thought saving money was the best thing to do, but I knew that the blurb and the cover of a book were the top two most important things of publishing. Do you all know why?" Several hands go up. I point to one in the front. "How about you? Woman in the pretty black skirt."

She stands as she's given a microphone and smiles widely. "Abigale," she says brightly. "We only have five seconds to sell a book. People really do judge a book by the cover. If the cover sucks, they aren't going to click on the book to read the blurb. If the blurb doesn't catch them, they won't consider buying the book."

I nod. "Mostly correct." I smile at her as she sits down with a confused, tilted head. "We have five seconds to interest people in clicking on our book to read the blurb. Most people won't click on the book if the cover is terrible or isn't catchy. Once we pull them in with that cover, then it's up to our blurb to reel them in. Catch them, if you will. In my case, my first book had a cover that wasn't terrible. But it really wasn't that great. I got some interest, but my blurb was awful. Anyone who bought the book, even though it sounded like a horrid and uninteresting book about Roman's, will forever be my best friends. I sold three books in the entire year I had it up. Three. And my page reads totaled only one thousand. In an entire year. Can anyone tell me if that's good or bad and why?" Every hand in the room shoots up. "Tan shirt in the back on the aisle near the door."

The older lady stands and smooths her skirt as she's handed a microphone. "Tiffani. Thank you for calling on me. It's not good. You put a lot of money into publishing and didn't make a single fraction of that back. The time and effort alone that it took you to write it made that not worth it all."

I nod again. "You're right. There are so many reasons my first book failed. Can anyone take a guess on what all of the things I did wrong are?" I switch to the next slide. It shows a full cover with my blurb for my flopped book. I take a deep breath and glance towards the side of the stage. Tyler is standing with his arms folded over his chest. He nods his encouragement. He knows how hard this is for me.

But it's really Lyric sitting in the audience between Matt and DJ that helps the most. She's been throwing me smiles, thumbs up signs, and small winks and nods throughout the entire hour I've been up here. She's not only being supportive, but she's being the calming force I need. Lyric is incredible and doesn't even know everything she's doing for me right now.

I point to a guy near the end in the back corner. "Yes, sir. In the black all the way at the back in the far corner."

He's handed a mic. "Eric." He squints after introducing himself. "I'd say your cover definitely isn't catchy. It's just an image of the Roman Colosseum. After reading your blurb, I'd guess your book is more of a historical romance. A retelling of Marc Antony's story in which he finds love, but the blurb sounds boring. It doesn't hint at any kind of conflict, and ruins the book by saying he takes over Rome from Caesar. I'd also venture to guess that you probably lost a lot of money in advertising on Amazon and social media. Since it was your first book, maybe you didn't have a newsletter or website to market yourself."

I nod as he hands the microphone off and sits down. "You're correct." I switch to the next slide. It shows everything I spent on the book and what I made. I look down at my notes while everyone studies the screen. "I spent nearly five grand during the year on advertising. As you can see, my Amazon ads didn't do very well. I spent just about ten dollars on the ads and got very little clicks. Less than a hundred. Most of my advertising was done on social media from my own personal accounts. I didn't have an author account. I didn't know what a newsletter was, so I didn't have one. I didn't get a website because I didn't think I needed one. I fell into the trap of thinking I was the shit. I dropped money on the cover. I thought my blurb was great. The only people who bought my book, though, was family. Distant family that I didn't send an autographed author copy to. The book was over 300 pages. So, my just over thousand reads were three people finishing the book and one not, or maybe a lot of people never finishing it." I see a hand shoot up next to Matt. I point to the small woman who looks to be in her sixties.

She stands and eagerly takes the microphone. "Hi. I'm Brenda. It looks like you have expenses for editing and formatting and proofing, but you mentioned you'd done that yourself."

I nod. "I had. But when I was trying to figure out why the book was failing so miserably, I noticed a lot of errors. It's difficult to edit yourself. Don't do it. No matter how much you think you know, you will miss things in your own work. I almost majored in English. I've been writing most of my life in some form or other, but you will never be able to edit yourself as well as someone else can. I searched for the best I could find and dropped three grand. The inside of my book looked incredible. But it didn't help because my book cover and blurb weren't interesting enough to drag people into it and hook them. It doesn't matter how much money you sink into your work. If you can't hook a reader and market it, you will never be able to find your success. So, going back to that first question. Yes. You have a very short amount of time to hook a reader. More like two seconds. And if they don't like the cover, it doesn't matter if your blurb is the greatest blurb ever written. You'll never get people there if that cover isn't stunning."

Lots of people murmur in agreement.

I smile and put a picture of the same book with a different cover and blurb. Next to it is what I've made since its relaunch. "This is the same book. It is being republished soon under a different name." I meet the eyes of the guy who asked about it in the first place. He's beaming, and it makes me smile.

I conclude my presentation and open it up for questions and answers. After nearly an hour of people asking me questions, I find my energy and my strength wavering. I'm gripping the podium once more in a death grip. I turn to Tyler and give him my signal to get me out of here. I've had enough. I hold his gaze and blink twice before turning away and answering one last question.

"What is the difference for you between traditional publishing and self-publishing? Do you recommend one over the other?" the young woman who can't be much more out of high school asks me.

I glance at Tyler as he walks onto the stage and stands respectfully behind me. Just his presence calms my racing heart. Lyric's eyes, full of concern, help keep me from shaking uncontrollably and running away. Matt and DJ help me to know I'm safe.

"Well, it honestly depends on you and your goals. For me, when I first started, I didn't have the time to do almost everything that needed to be done to be successful as a self-published author. I was working a full-time, corporate job at the time. I also had no idea what publishing entailed. After the year I had given myself as a self-published author was done, I unpublished my book and said I'd never make it. That doesn't have to be you, but you do need to understand that self-publishing is a slow process, and you need to do everything on your own. Or hire a PA who can run your social media and help you to promote yourself. You need to become familiar with ads. Keywords that work and those that don't. You need to learn all about targeting so your book is placed in the best areas. You'll need to decide if you want to go wide or if you want to be exclusive to Amazon, which is the largest book retailer in the world."

Her eyes widen. "Even bigger than Barnes 'N' Noble?"

I nod and tamp down the lump forming in my throat. I need to end this, but I don't want to leave her question unanswered. "Being an author means never stopping your marketing strategy or self-promotion strategy. Even if you do get a publisher, which isn't easy, you still need to market yourself and promote yourself. You still need to be present to your readers and approachable in some manners. To answer your question, traditional publishing worked best for me because I was clueless. The education you're all able to get now wasn't available to me when I started. I sent my manuscript to numerous publishing companies and got rejected by all of them. I self-published and failed. When I left the corporate world, I focused solely on writing. I finished an entire series before sending out a new manuscript. I got rejected again by everyone, except one. The one I hadn't sent to before because I was intimidated by just how big they are. They took a chance and saw a diamond in the rough sea of authors. My agent is incredible and got me the best deal that included the publisher marketing me and my agent helping me with all of that self-promotion. Not all publishers do that. You have to fight for it. I think that, right there, is the entire point of being an author. Fight for what you want. Fight for your work and yourself. Never settle for less than the best because you are worth absolutely nothing less than the best." I nod and take a step back, still gripping the podium. I sway slightly.

Tyler is right there to steady me. Just like he always is when I do these things. Steady, sturdy Tyler. He grips my hips and moves me to his side and slightly behind him, keeping his arm down for me to grip as I hide and use his pine and naturally fresh scent to calm me. I catch Lyric's eyes. She's looking at me worriedly and chewing on her bottom lip furiously.

Tyler leans down to the microphone as several more people's hands shoot up with more questions they want answered. "Thank you everyone for coming to see Mariah Marie's speech at this year's convention. We hope she taught you a lot of things you can take with you on your own journey. Mariah will be doing a book signing tomorrow afternoon. Don't forget to grab a leaflet on your way out that will let you know what room she'll be in for the book signing and all of the things she'll be offering all of her attendees. I hear she'll be giving away a lot of freebies to get you excited for her new upcoming release, so don't miss out!" He stands to his full height and gives everyone a wave as they stand and applaud.

As he always does, he takes my hand, letting me grip it as tightly as possible, and leads me off the stage. He uses his body to block my view of everyone as tunnel vision sets in. All I can see now is the side of the stage. Safety. I can hear nothing more than the roaring of my own blood in my ears. The panic is setting in, and I'm powerless to stop it.

I feel myself being set down in a chair, but I've long ago closed my eyes and let Tyler lead me, trusting him completely to get me out of there. I feel a head fall into my lap and arms encircle my waist, hugging me tightly. Hands fall to my shoulders. There's another on my thigh.

"Look at me, Mariah," DJ's deep voice says. So calmly. Soothing.

I take a breath and try to steady my breathing as I slowly open my eyes. Lyric is kneeling at my side. Her head is in my lap against my stomach. She's hugging me hard. Matt and Tyler are both at my sides with their hands on my shoulders. DJ is kneeling directly in front of me, gently gripping my thigh. I focus on all of them and the comfort they provide.

"You're okay, Rih," DJ says to me, keeping his green eyes on mine. "Breathe in through your nose and out through your mouth."

I nod and do as he says. I'm not sure if it's his commands, or Matt and Tyler flanking each of my sides and rubbing my shoulders, or if it's Lyric wrapped around me. I feel myself start to calm before I reach the point of true panic, so whatever the reason, none of them will ever know how grateful I am.

The only person near me who has ever seen me panic truly is Tyler. It's why we have a secret signal. He knows when I'm getting near the point of no return and will swoop in to save me. I've never let anyone else see that vulnerability before him.

Until today.

I let out a long breath. "I thought I was getting better with it," I say quietly. I close my eyes and shake my head. "I really thought I was doing okay again."

"Mariah, stop. We've talked about this," Tyler says. He squeezes my shoulder. "It's a long and hard road. You are improving. When I first met you, doing what you just did would never have happened. Not a chance in all of the Hells."

"Rih, I watched you up there. You did incredible," DJ says with a grin. "You got through it. And now, you get to go upstairs and relax with your girl."

"We can order room service," Lyric says quietly. She kisses my thigh, and I calm even more.

"I'm sure Tyler would love to cancel dinner plans tonight," Matt says.

"I'm happy to. I'll even order room service for you." Tyler leans down and kisses the top of my head.

"I'd like that." I nod. "A lot."

"You need to come down," Matt says. "DJ and I will even be quiet tonight."

Lyric giggles. "We beat you in that battle, and you know it."

"Fuck, I can't even argue with you and say we did. You two got fucking loud." DJ laughs.

"I don't want to know what the hell any of that means," Tyler says. He leans down and kisses the top of my head. "I'll take care of room service. Are you going to be okay? I have a couple of calls I need to make about tomorrow and the marketing supplies. I was supposed to get them delivered today, but they were delayed. I have someone picking them up from L.A."

I look up at him, expecting to feel some kind of panic at not having supplies for tomorrow's book signing, but I know Tyler. He's never once failed on getting things we need when we need them. I know he'll take care of this just like he always does. That thought soothes me so much.

After I've calmed a little more, Matt and DJ lead us to our room. When a couple more men step into the elevator with us, I jump a little before realizing it's our security. I'd forgotten completely they have been with us because they are incredible at blending in and not crowding us. They have a suite on the same floor as us across the hall from ours so they're near. They always sweep our room before they let us be alone, but they're so fast, while thorough, that we barely notice when they leave.

Today is no different. As soon as they're done, they both nod and slip out the door. I collapse on the couch and look up at Lyric. She's still looking at me worriedly and chewing her lower lip. It just makes me want to lick it. Or her. I'd be okay with either.

But I try to be a little firm. I'm not the most dominant of people, but I know Lyric is far more submissive than I am and needs some type of guidance. Thanks to all of my long conversations with DJ about her, I have ideas on how to do just that.

I hold out a hand for her. She shuffles towards me, still chewing on her lip. It's one of the things she has been trying to fix, but she starts doing it whenever she's nervous about something or doesn't know how to do something or help with something. She hates it because it always ends up hurting her, but she can't figure out a way to make herself not do it.

She takes my hand and sniffles, still chewing on her lip. I slowly turn her around so her back is to me. She gives me a confused look over her shoulder when I grip her hips and stop her from moving any farther.

Lyric is a truly beautiful woman. The simple yellow t-shirt she's wearing with the black jeggings shows off sinful curves that I'm pretty sure she doesn't have any idea she has and just what they do to me. I lean forward and sink my teeth into her perfect ass.

She squeaks and jumps, looking down at me in surprise. "What was that for?"

"Lip biting. You said you wanted to stop and that you're having a hard time."

She tilts her head. "So, you bit me?"

I shrug as I take her hand. I lean back and pull her down next to me. "I'm not good at spankings. I know you're…" I trail off and squint my eyes as I think. "Submissive? DJ said you all have talked at length about why relationships never work for you. He said it's because you are submissive and most women can't give you the things you need. He said he and Matt help to ground you when you feel like you're out of control, but most women can't do that. I didn't have any idea what he meant. He said spankings. Not that he and Matt spank you. He said they more just help you by making sure you keep on a schedule. And that they are good about talking to you, like DJ did to me today."

She cuddles into my side and tucks her feet under her. She draws patterns on my thigh as I hug her. "I have this thing with staying up to read when I have a bad day. Then, I get to work and have an even worse day because I didn't sleep. So, I'll end up getting very little sleep for a few days. DJ and Matt have started to pick up on when I do that, so they have me stay at their house. Which is okay because Magni loves playing with his pack. But while I'm there it's like they…" She trails off as she thinks of the words. "Reprogram me. They have me up at a certain time. They have me in bed at a certain time. They keep me on a schedule with eating and everything. Then, I'm okay for a while. Matt did actually spank me once when I was out of control. I mean, I was talking so bad about myself after a call. I really felt like I messed up." She falls silent.

"What happened on the call?" I ask her after a few moments.

She sighs. "It was a suicide call. I was the first person there. At first, she wasn't really making threats or anything, but she wouldn't open her bedroom door. I called in our CIT team, a critical incident team. They're called in for things like a mental health crisis. Anyway, I know now that calling them in and waiting was the right thing to do. I kept talking to her while we waited, but she fell silent. She didn't give me any kind of indication that she was planning on doing anything. She didn't answer me after a couple of minutes. I got super nervous. I tried to get into her room, but the door was locked. I tried kicking it in. It didn't budge. By the time we got the door kicked down, we'd discovered she had pushed her giant dresser in front of the door, and her bed in front of that."

"Oh…"

Lyric sniffles and wipes her eyes. "I was riddled with guilt. I went over everything I could have done differently. In the end, though, she had slit her wrists. There was nothing we could do. She'd done it before I had gotten there, and bled out while she was talking to me." She cuddles closer. "I took it really hard. After a few days, I was truly just… distraught. I had decided to quit. I thought I was a terrible cop. How can I be a good cop when I couldn't even save a sixteen-year-old girl's life? I spiraled pretty far. I wasn't eating or sleeping. I had missed a shift without calling in. DJ and Matt both came over to my house that day. They'd been keeping in contact with me on the phone, but I wanted time alone. My partner, Blake, went to them and told them he thought I needed an intervention. He'd also been in contact with me. He came over before Matt and DJ did and saw how awful I looked. He went to them."

"And they helped you?" My grip on her tightens. I hate that she had to go through that. It makes my heart hurt.

"They did. Matt mostly. I was really upset and wasn't listening at all to anyone. Matt actually warned me a few times that he didn't give a shit if he was my friend, my Lieutenant, my older brother, or however the hell else I thought of him. He would spank me if I didn't stop saying I was terrible, and that I should have stopped it. But it was when I said it should have been me that he didn't hesitate."

"Oh my God, babe…" I hug her closer. "I hate that you felt that way."

"Matt spanked me. Hard. I haven't spiraled like that since, but I know he'd do it again if I ever got to that point. I'm glad that they were there. I'm glad Matt did what he did. It brought me back to reality. It's hard to explain, but I needed it. I needed it to ground me. Bring me back."

I nod. "I understand. I'm not really all that dominant, but DJ helped me see how I can get around that when it comes to you. I'd never be able to spank you, but I can do things like keep you on track. When I told him I'd never be able to dole out a punishment, he said a punishment didn't have to be a spanking. It could be a nip or bite. So…" I smile a little and kiss her head, burying my nose in her hair.

She giggles. "So, you bit me."

I giggle. "Yep."

"It was effective."

"Good."

Lyric and I shift so we're both comfortable. After a few minutes, Lyric takes out her phone. One of the things I've come to love so much about Lyric is that we can cuddle just like this without saying anything and be perfectly content. I love everything about her, but sometimes, the way we can be silent together and get lost in just being with each other is one of my favorite things.

I love holding her and playing with her hair while she reads, like she is right now, or we watch a movie. I've never been in a serious relationship with anyone, at least not on this level of intimacy, but I could definitely get used to this.

No. Not this.

Her.

I could get used to being like this with her.

Chapter Twelve

☆ *Lyric* ☆

I slow to a walk a block before the MGM and look at my watch on my wrist that tells me my heart rate.

"That was the best run I've had in a while," my bodyguard says.

I've come to really like Adam. He's truly fun to be around. We've become friends over the past couple weeks since I met him. I can see that friendship continuing long after Mariah and I go back home.

I smile as he falls in step next to me. "I run every morning, but the runs this past week have been some of my best. I think it's because I have someone to run with me." I bump him with my shoulder.

He laughs. "I usually just hit the treadmill in my home gym. It's been nice getting out and running in the fresh air. Even if Vegas is fucking a hundred times hotter than New York. I'll take New York any day."

I don't know why this causes me to giggle, but it does. "You definitely don't seem like a Vegas kind of dude."

"Hell no. I'd go crazy here. The weather is just one factor. The fucking insanity is another. People just walking down the streets with booze? What the hell possesses people to act like jackasses when they're on vacation?"

"You'd hate Gainesville. We're a college town. Bar closing gets pretty crazy."

"No thank you. I'm good." He grins as we near the hotel.

My eyes widen. "Blake?" My eyes fall on the tall, rather gorgeous man in front of me near the entrance to the MGM.

"Blake?" Adam asks with his voice lowered. I can tell he's very much on guard.

"My partner. From Gainesville."

Blake grins a dashing smile. "Hey, partner. You miss me?" He holds out his arms for a hug.

I don't know why, but I hesitate before stepping into them. "Yeah. How was your vacation?"

"Good. Peaceful. Can't wait to go back, but I thought I'd come out here and see how Vegas is behaving. How's Mariah? You two getting along?" He drops his arms as I step away.

I cross my arms over my chest and unconsciously step slightly behind Adam. My wariness slams into me. I hadn't told him anything about Mariah. I haven't talked to him much over the past couple of weeks. Blake was on vacation when I met Mariah at that call.

I hadn't told him I was going to New York with her. I just told him that I was taking some time off. When he checked in with me via text, I had just been telling him things are going well. Mariah never once came up because I wasn't sure what we were to each other, or where this thing we have going on was heading.

"How did you know about Mariah?" I ask quietly. "I hadn't mentioned her because I wasn't really sure what we were to each other."

He shakes his head and raises an eyebrow. "You know I work at the same department as you. People talk." He laughs. "Why didn't you tell me, though? We're partners."

I hug myself and take a breath. "You're right. I'm sorry. I'm just on edge. There's been a lot going on that I haven't had a chance to tell you. Um… Want to come upstairs? Mariah is probably getting ready for her book signing. You can meet her while I take a shower."

He grins. "Yeah. I'd love to." His eyes fall on Adam. "Who's this guy?"

"Oh. This is Adam. He's part of that long story. I'll explain upstairs. I'm starving and sweaty." I shiver. "Gross."

"Okay. I'm Blake." He sticks out his hand for Adam to shake.

Adam doesn't take it. "No offense, man, but I don't shake hands. One of the easiest ways to get my ass kicked. The Marines trained me well."

Blake slowly drops his hand. He looks slightly nervous. "Marines, huh? You know, our Lieutenant was a Marine. He's the trainer for the department. He deals with all of our refresher courses. Fighting and all."

Adam nods. "Once a Marine. Always a Marine." He takes out his phone.

Blake's nervousness shows a little more. I'm suddenly even more on edge. Blake shifts from one foot to the other and crosses his arms over his chest as he watches Adam. "Got a hot date?" he jokes. But he doesn't take his eyes off Adam's phone.

"Nope."

I glance at his phone and see he's texting someone, but I don't say anything. I clear my throat. "Are you hungry?" I ask Blake. "The restaurant is incredible. Mariah and I could just meet you down there." I don't know why, but Blake is making me so nervous that the idea of him being near me or Mariah in our suite scares me. I've never in my life been nervous around Blake. He's my partner. I trust him with my life. He's always had my six.

"Nah. I can wait." Blake smiles, but he doesn't look at me.

I watch as his right hand falls to his waist. His elbow rests on something so naturally. His stance changes. He widens his legs just slightly. I know instinctively his gun is in a holster on his hip. He never carries his off-duty weapon on his hip. Blake prefers to have it on his ankle. I've never understood his reasoning for that. He's always said it's because it's less obvious. Less conspicuous. I've always thought that it was just harder to get to if it was ever needed.

Adam is really good at his job, though, and takes my nervousness as a sign that something is wrong. His stance has changed completely. I can tell he's ready to fight if he needs to. I thank God for him. I may be a police officer, but Blake is a big guy. I'm not armed. We train a lot together. I know what he's capable of.

I hope that everything I'm feeling is just nerves. I feel like a war is being waged inside me because Blake isn't someone I should fear. He's my partner. Friend. Blake has never given me any kind of reason to be afraid of him. He's one of the first people I'd turn to if I needed any kind of help. So, why I feel the way I do right now makes me feel like the stress is getting to me.

I shake my head. I'm being crazy. This is Blake. My partner on the streets ever since I started working for Gainesville Police Department. Blake is a player. He goes through more women than anyone I know, but he's a solid cop. He's a good guy. Good friend. He's one of the good people out there. Fighting the good fight every single day alongside me and all of our other partners.

I rub my eyes. "Okay. Let's get going then. The sweat is sticking to me, and I feel icky."

"We need to rush this," Adam says. I look up at him. Blake levels him with a glare. Adam doesn't flinch or take his eyes off Blake. "Tyler says breakfast in ten minutes. It would be best if you just stayed down in the lobby. We'll meet you there on the way to breakfast."

I realize Adam is giving me a way to keep Blake out of our room. I give him an almost imperceptible smile as my eyes flick back to Blake. "He's right. It's okay. We'll be down in a few minutes. We can catch up then." I start walking towards the door as Adam begins moving. I make sure to stay on the side furthest from Blake.

But it's pointless.

Like a flash of lightning, Blake's arm snakes around my waist. He pulls me to his chest at the same time he pistol-whips Adam in the side of the head. I scream as I try to push myself away from Blake, but I know I'm not going anywhere no matter what I do. Blake was trained by the best, just as I was. Lieutenant Matt Chance doesn't fuck around when it comes to officer safety.

"Fuck!" Adam yells as he stumbles back. He doesn't fall, though. Not until Blake hits him with the butt of his gun on the other side of his head. Adam drops to his knees.

I look around. There has to be someone who sees what is going on. But the sun has barely risen. It's early. I always do my runs early before it gets too warm. There's no one out here. Not even security or valet.

Blake pulls me with him inside the hotel. He presses the gun against my back. "Don't scream. Don't make a scene. I will never hurt you, Lyric. I love you. That's why I'm doing this. For us. But I will fucking kill anyone who tries to interfere. You don't want that. I've stood by and watched you with others for long enough."

It's like everything around me just stops as he speaks. "W-what?" He loves me? What the hell is happening? My head is spinning. My heart feels like it's going to pound out of my chest.

"You heard me." Blake propels me towards the elevators. "Which one?"

I'm in a state of shock and just point. He shoves me towards the elevator that leads to our floor and forces me to use my keycard to open the doors. When they do, he pushes me in. I'm starting to hyperventilate. I grip my chest. My eyes fall on Adam. He's running full speed towards the elevator, but I know he won't make it.

Especially when Blake raises his gun and points it at Adam.

I push his arm away just as the doors close. "No! I'm cooperating! Don't shoot him!" I scream at him, finally finding my voice. Though, how is something I'll have to revisit if I survive this.

Blake looks down at me as the elevator starts moving. "Are you fucking him? Please tell me you aren't fucking him."

I shake my head. "Blake, you know I like women. You've helped me pick up a few! What is wrong with you?" My tears are starting to blind me. I wipe them away furiously.

"Me? What's wrong with me? I've fucking been in love with you for years, Lyric! And you could never see it. Fucking others when you could have been fucking me! Someone else always got in the way!" He grips my shoulders and shoves me. My back hits the wall of the elevator, causing the car to shake.

I let out a whimper and terrified squeak. I push him. I scratch, claw, and kick, but Blake's solid as steel, six feet five form doesn't budge a single centimeter. I scream, but his hands only find their way around my neck. He squeezes just enough to cut off my air. My hands fly to his as my eyes widen in shock. I scratch them, but he doesn't let up his grip.

"You are going to be mine, Lyric. Fucking know that. I'm done fucking around. I'm done pretending to be in love with a bitch I have no feelings for. And I certainly won't let fucking Mariah fucking Marie, author extraordinaire, stand in my way of having the one woman in this world meant for me. You're mine. Fucking mine, Lyric. Do you understand me?"

My air supply is getting less and less. I nod because if I don't, I feel like he'll kill me. I know he'll kill me. There's no doubt in my mind.

Looking into his brown eyes tells me all I need to know. He is dead serious and won't hesitate to kill anyone who stands in his way.

His grip lets up on my neck. "You're going to do everything I tell you. Not because you want to, but because you're a submissive. You'll do what you're told because it's who you are. You don't want me to hurt anyone. Do you?"

I shake my head. Tears fall uncontrollably now. He's right. I don't want him to hurt anyone. I'll do anything to make sure he doesn't. Especially the woman I love. I'm in love with Mariah. I'll do anything he wants me to so long as he leaves her alone.

"I don't," I whisper.

"Such a good girl."

The elevator doors open. Blake yanks me and spins me so I'm in front of him and my back is firmly against his chest. The gun digs into my back once more. He shoves me ahead of him, checking the hall for anyone before he pushes me out.

"Room," he demands.

I briefly contemplate bringing him to Matt and DJ's room, but my key wouldn't work. He'd catch on right away to what I'm doing. And if I got lucky and Matt or DJ opened the door, Blake might shoot them. I don't want anyone hurt. So, I lead him to our room. I have a better chance of getting him to leave Mariah alone if I do everything he says.

Adam knows what's happening. He has a key to our room. He was okay. He can help. I just need to stall. I need to keep Blake with me and talking until Adam can get to us and help. He'll sound the alarm. He'll get backup. I have to believe that because if I don't, Blake will hurt someone. He'll hurt Mariah. I can't let him hurt Mariah. I don't care what he does to me. Just not Mariah.

I use my key to open the door as the tears fall. I pray with everything I am to whoever is listening that Mariah is not in this room. I hope that somehow Adam got the message to Quinn, Mariah's bodyguard. I hope he got her out.

When I open the door, I catch a glimpse of someone ducking behind the door to our bedroom. The tears fall faster. She's in here. Mariah is in here. I sob harder and feel myself losing any and all strength I had that was keeping me going just moments before. I would take the bullet for

Mariah if I had to, but there is no one to stop him from getting to her after I'm gone.

"Good girl," Blake says, shoving me into the room and slamming the door behind him. "Nice room. That Mariah bitch has more money than I thought to afford a place that probably costs a grand a night."

"Seven hundred, actually," a dangerously deep, very protective male voice says from behind me just as arms grab me around the waist and shove me hard towards the bedroom.

I don't bother looking behind me. I know by the scent who shoved me towards the room.

Matt.

"Goddamn hell!" Blake screams.

"Don't fucking move!" Matt yells.

I lose my balance and fall to my knees. I scramble the rest of the way to the bedroom and slam the door behind me. I look around as I quickly stand up, but Mariah isn't here. I grip my chest. My heart feels like it's shattering. Like I'm having a heart attack.

Behind the closed door is chaos.

Crashing.

Breaking.

Screaming.

"Get the fuck off me!" Blake yells.

"Stop fucking moving!" DJ screams. Oh my God. Thank God DJ is there to back Matt up.

More crashing.

"Get off me!" Blake yells again.

Something shatters. There are framed photographs on the wall. I'm sure they've been broken by someone's back.

Or head.

My eyes fall on the bathroom door as it opens just a crack. Mariah pokes her head out and waves me over to her.

"Oh, fuck," I whisper through my tears as I run to her. She silently closes the door behind me and pulls me onto the floor with her. We wrap ourselves around each other as silent tears fall and quiet sobs rack our bodies.

"I'm okay," she whispers into my neck, now soaked with her tears.

"I love you," I whisper back. "I love you so much. I don't care if it's only been two weeks. I love you." My nails dig into her back and the back of her neck as I hug her.

"I love you, too," she whispers, holding me just as tightly.

We both jump when we hear another crash. Like someone is being slammed into the wall or table. There's more yelling. Screaming.

"Gun! Gun! He's got a gun!" Quinn yells.

We both choke back screams when shots ring out. Someone howls in pain.

More yelling from the other room.

"I'll fucking kill you!" Blake screams. "She's fucking mine! Got that? Mine! And that bitch Mariah is done. Fucking done coming between me and what's mine!"

"Drop the gun! Drop the fucking gun!" DJ commands.

A barrage of bullets.

We hold each other as tightly as possible whispering silent prayers.

"Please let Matt and DJ be okay," I whisper into Mariah's hair.

"Please let Adam and Quinn be okay," Mariah whispers into my shoulder.

Mariah and I don't let each other go as we continue whispering our silent pleas to whoever is listening. God. Satan. I don't fucking care. I'd happily sell my soul to the devil himself if it means my family, friends, and girl are safe.

But when someone starts pounding on the door to the bathroom, I'm certain we aren't going to be that lucky. So, I do what anyone would do before they die. I hold onto the love of my life with everything I am and thank God I had the time with her I did. I thank him for showing me what true happiness is.

What true love is.

Epilogue

☆ Mariah ☆

(One Year Later)

I sway with Lyric as we both look at the epic scenery before us. The Norwegian Fjords is truly everything it's cracked up to be. Everything I've imagined it is and more since Lyric told me about it one year ago.

A whole year.

A year since Justice was killed.

A year since my best friend was so very cruelly taken from me.

An entire year since fate paved the road to the love of my life and the greatest friends I've ever had. She took everything from me only to build me back up and give me everything I've ever dreamed of and so very much more.

She gave me a family.

For a long time, all I had was Tyler and my family at Alexander's Publishing House. After I left Duluth and that corporate world behind to follow my dream and be who I am, everyone abandoned me. It was part of the reason I kept who I am from Tyler for so long and only went to certain places to pick up my dates. Places no one knew me. I didn't want to lose everything again because of who I choose to sleep with and love.

Apparently, fate, though she's a very fickle being, had other plans for me. And those plans were Lyric, the love I've searched my whole life for. The unconditional love that so many want and never find. The kind of love I write about.

Her plans included Matt, DJ, and Tyler. The family I've always wanted, but never quite got. The family who accepts me for who I am, and supports me and my dreams. The family that loves and protects me no matter what.

"I miss my wolf. I'm sitting here looking at all of this beautiful scenery and thinking how my brother and dad would love all of this, and all I can think of is Magni and how much I miss him."

I kiss Lyric's neck with a smile. "I miss Loki, too, but I'm sure they're enjoying themselves running around Mr. Alexander's yard."

Lyric giggles. "I can't believe a big house like that fits in New York. I mean, I thought Matt and DJ had a big place. You could fit three of their houses and yards on Mr. Alexander's property."

I laugh. "I know. Which is how I know Loki, Magni, Valkyrie, and Tyr are having a ball and probably won't want to come home."

Lyric laughs. "Well, too bad for them. I refuse to live in New York. I'm a Florida girl."

"Me, too. I love New York for a few days. Then I hate it."

I rest my cheek against hers as we enjoy the peaceful moment; the majestic landscape laid out before us. A peacefulness that we both need after the events of just one year ago. Events that changed both of our lives forever.

As I hug my girl tightly and stand admiring everything around us, I allow myself to think about how we got here.

Blake.

Officer Blake Ericson.

I didn't know it at the time, but Blake was pretending to be someone else. The entire time he was dating Justice, he had been lying. We don't know exactly why, but we all have ideas that make quite a bit of sense.

Lyric.

Ever since Lyric started at the department, she'd been assigned as his partner. He'd fallen for her, but she's been fairly open about her sexuality. He knew she was interested in women. Not men. Not him. Though, he did flirt shamelessly with her. Lyric always thought it was just fun and games. He knew he couldn't have her but loved teasing her. Loved the flirting. The relationship. What she didn't know was that he was serious about it. His feelings for her only grew, despite the fact that she didn't want him.

We found out that though Blake had been dating Justice for a long time, he had been hiding his identity from her because he didn't want her to know about his feelings and shameless flirting with Lyric and most of the rest of Gainesville's female population. Blake had been sleeping around for years.

He'd also been threatening women and forcing them to sleep with him. None of them came forward because of who he was. A cop. He had told them all that no one would believe them. He was a well-liked police officer and made all of them feel like nothing more than sluts. According to the numerous women who came forward over the past year, Blake made them all believe that the department would side with him and not ever believe the word of a whore.

It's a side that no one who worked with Blake saw. He wasn't lying when he said he was well-liked. No one in the department had a bad thing to say about him. Not even Lyric, who was the target of a lot of his twisted games. I didn't know it. Neither did Matt and DJ. Lyric, however, told us that a lot of her shifts for years began with something slipped into her locker calling her a lesbian whore. Graphic images of two women in sexual positions with red X's through the picture.

Blake was always the one who comforted her. He'd promised her he'd take care of it. And he did. Or so she thought. After he made the promise, everything stopped for a while. But they would start right back up again. Blake would swoop in and be the hero. Hug her while she cried. Make her feel safe. So safe, in fact, that she didn't bother telling Matt or DJ about any of it, even though the two are the only family she has. She didn't feel like she needed to because Blake helped her deal with it.

Blake had woven such a tight web of lies that when it came to Justice and his reason for killing her, Matt and DJ had no motive at all. Not until I found her journal. I was cleaning out my SUV, the one I wrecked, of personal belongings before it was taken to a wreckage yard. Under one of the seats, was a journal I'd never seen. There was a note on the very last page that said if anything ever happened to her, it would be her boyfriend that had done it.

The entire journal was filled with things she'd never told me. She'd been collecting evidence against Blake. She'd found out his true identity about a year before and was writing down everything she discovered in her journal.

She said in the journal she became suspicious of him because there were so many nights he wasn't around. She thought he was cheating and started following him when he left her house before dinner. Lyric and Blake worked several night shifts for overtime, but Blake worked far more of them than she did. Justice followed him to the police department and watched until she saw him leaving in a squad car in full uniform.

It's how we knew about the sexual assaults. Not only had he lied to her about what he actually did for a job, but he also used his uniform to lure women into his trap. The night she followed him, at least the first time, she took pictures and taped them to the pages of the journal. She followed him several other nights and took more pictures. But she knew that pictures could say something else. Something that may not be the truth. So, she also took video. She taped a flash drive inside the journal as well. It was with that video that she knew she had him.

She said in her journal's last entry that she was going to come to my house for dinner and pick up the journal she'd hidden. She was going to tell me everything and ask me to go with her to turn everything into the police.

She was killed because he found out she was going to the police about him with all of the evidence she had. But he didn't know she'd installed cameras or anything in her house. He had no idea that she'd done it to protect herself just in case he figured out what she was doing. He told her before he killed her that he saw her following him. He took her laptop after he killed her, probably thinking she wouldn't have saved the video she took anywhere else. It was found when his house was searched after he disappeared.

Matt and DJ never told us they knew it was Blake because they didn't think he had any idea where we were. They didn't want to alarm us. We didn't know they'd been talking to Adam and Quinn. It's the entire reason Adam immediately texted Quinn as soon as he laid his eyes on Blake.

The only time Justice had the opportunity to put the journal into my vehicle was the day before when we'd had coffee, and I took her home because she had a flat tire. According to the video and audio the police had from her surveillance system, Blake knew what she'd done and what she planned to do. He believed she'd told me. It was the reason I became a target. He told her before he killed her that I was next.

But it all came back to Lyric, and his obsession with her. When they searched his house, they found videos of her on his laptop. Videos of her changing and showering in her home. They found out he had cameras in her home. Cameras in her shower, bathroom, bedroom, every single room in her house. There were videos of her getting off with toys or her fingers. Videos of her watching videos while she got off.

He had videos of both male and female voices commanding her to come. Lyric believed that what he had said to her in the elevator made much more sense after she'd learned that. She thinks he believed she couldn't be a lesbian if she could get off to a male voice telling her to come.

He had some of her clothing in the top drawer of his dresser. Panties she had no idea he had. Clothing she doesn't know how he took. He had things that she'd never seen before that we figured he thought she'd like when he finally did make his move.

To Lyric he was a good guy. He was a hero. At least that's how he portrayed himself to her. He didn't want his image in her eyes to be ruined. He knew if Justice went to the police and turned him in, his entire life would be over. But most of all, he'd lose Lyric. Lyric was his end game. Whether she wanted to be or not, he felt like he could convince her.

At least that's the way Lyric felt when he had her in the elevator. She felt like he believed he could convince her to be with him and love him the way he thought he loved her. We've all come to the conclusion that he's not capable of love. He's a sociopath. The world is better without him.

When Lyric opened the door of the hotel suite we were in while in Las Vegas, she had no idea that Adam had sounded the alarm. He'd texted Quinn while they were still talking to Blake. By the time Blake got Lyric to the elevator, Quinn had already gotten Matt and DJ. They all came to our room and told me that I needed to go into the bedroom. DJ said when he gave me the signal to run to the bathroom.

I didn't ask questions. I just did as I was told, trusting that I'd learn what was going on afterwards. When I saw the door to our suite open and Lyric shoved through it, I intentionally kept my eyes on DJ. I couldn't look at Lyric because I knew I'd run out of the room towards her. I forced myself to trust the three people in the room would take care of her.

When DJ gave me the signal, I ran to the bathroom and closed the door. But I saw Matt grab Lyric and practically throw her into the room. I waited until I had heard her close the door before I opened the bathroom one because it's what DJ said to do.

Lyric and I sat holding each other in the bathroom for what felt to me like hours. We whispered to each other how much we loved each other. We said quiet prayers to anyone listening to protect those we loved.

When it was all over, Matt, DJ, and Quinn all shot Blake after he fired on them. He hit Quinn in the leg. A millimeter to the left and Quinn may not be here today. He would have probably bled out because the bullet was that close to an artery. One of the bullets skimmed Matt's arm. Blake was killed.

Adam didn't wait for the elevator to come back down. There's only one elevator that went to our floor. He ran up the stairs. When he got to the room, he'd heard all of the commotion and yelling. Just as he was about to enter the room, the first shot rang out.

Tyler came out of his room across the hall next to our security's room when he heard the yelling. When the shot rang out, he ran for the room. Adam stopped him, thankfully. I can't imagine what would have happened if either Adam or Tyler had gone in. Chaos and confusion would have ensued. Blake could have hurt any one of them if he'd taken advantage of the distraction. I'm glad that Adam thought to keep Tyler away. I don't know what I would have done if I had lost any of them that day.

When it was all over, though, and the dust settled, Lyric and I were closer than ever. And every single day since, we've grown far stronger as a couple. We knew in that bathroom how we felt about each other. If we're being honest, we knew much sooner than that. It was love at first sight with me and Lyric. Something I never believed in until her.

We were engaged to be married just six months after we met. And we got married only a month after that in a small, and very private, ceremony in DJ's and Matt's backyard. The only people in attendance were DJ, Matt, our wolves, Tyler, Adam, Quinn, and Baron Alexander, who refused to miss the wedding of the woman he considers a daughter, something I never knew until then.

"I'm so happy I got my happily ever after," I whisper against Lyric's neck as the last of the sun sinks down behind the horizon. "My pretty cop."

She blushes and hugs my arms close to her body. "It was something I never thought I'd find, but always held out hope for. I'm so glad it's you."

I kiss her neck and stand, letting my hands trail a fiery blaze down her body until they reach her hips. A quiet moan escapes her beautiful, full lips as she turns to me. I take her hands and kiss her before turning and leading her back to our cabin on the ship. We have to meet DJ and Matt soon for dinner, but I really want my pretty cop.

Lyric follows shyly behind me. I open our door when we reach it and lead her inside, closing it and locking it behind us. Unable to resist her anymore, I lose all my restraint. I kiss her with all of the pent up passion I've been stockpiling all day. I tangle my fingers in her hair when she moans and use my body to pin her against the wall as I suck on her tongue.

I pull back slowly. "Yummy."

She blinks up at me, dazed. I push off the wall and her, instantly missing the contact, and lead her to the bed. We both eagerly strip off our clothes on the way. Less for us to do when we get there, and more time for me to enjoy her.

I climb onto the bed and pull her with me. I gently lay her down and settle between her legs. I allow my eyes to roam all over hers. Worship her as she deserves to be. Like the Goddess my beautiful girl is.

"You know, when you look at me like that, I have to fight myself from mauling you." Lyric's smile could melt hearts all over the world. Thank God it's reserved just for me.

I lower myself to her center. Usually, I'd spend time kissing her and getting her ready for me. But not today. Today, I just need her. I need to taste her. Love her. I need to make her come and see her pleasure to calm my pounding heart. Thinking about how I almost lost her always makes me just want to show her how much she means to me. To be close to her.

I smile and lick her clit. "I know. It's the same feeling I get for you when you look at me like you want to devour me."

She moans at the feel of my tongue against her soft and silky skin. She's already so wet for me. She wraps my long hair around her hand and tugs me into her pussy as she arches. It's quite obvious that she needs to come. She only takes control and pulls me closer to her when she's already so close.

I suck her clit into my mouth and moan low, sending vibrations through her clit as I slide two fingers into her soaked pussy. She nearly collapses around me. Her pussy pulses erratically as I start to thrust while I suck her clit and flick it with my tongue.

"Oh, fuck, yes, Mariah." Lyric starts sliding herself over my fingers. I spread my fingers and thrust harder, deeper, and faster just like she likes it. I crook my fingers against her and feel her clench uncontrollably around my fingers.

"Mmm…," I moan again. "God, I love the way you taste."

"Oh, Mariah, I'm… so close… I'm -" Lyric's thighs tremble as she thrusts her hips against my tongue and fingers. "Mariah! I need to come for you!"

"Come for me, my love. Let me taste you." I swirl my tongue around her clit and keep thrusting inside her with my fingers. I twist them just as she starts to come.

"Ah! Mariah! Fuck, yes!" She pulls me closer to her pussy as her hips jerk. She rides her release while I lavish her and lick all she gives me until she's clean.

When she starts to come down, she loosens her grip on my hair. I slowly crawl up her body, leaving light kisses along the way, until I reach her lips. I tangle my fingers in her hair and smile as I lean down to kiss her. She won't admit it to anyone but me, but Lyric loves her own taste just as much as she loves mine.

"I love making you come," I whisper as I slowly pull away. "There's just something about you that makes coming look so hot and beautiful."

She blushes and turns her head. "So do you."

I kiss her neck before I slowly get up. "We should probably get ready for dinner. I think DJ hates lateness almost as much as Tyler."

Lyric looks up at me with a devilish smile and sexy glimmer in her eyes. "We have time." She sits up and pounces, knocking me back onto the bed.

I let out a squeak and giggle as she pins me. "That was adorable."

Lyric smiles and kisses me. As I had just done to her, leaving kisses on my way up her body, she gives me the same treatment and leaves kisses on her way down my body. She licks my pussy slowly and nips my clit. I jerk into her mouth with a moan.

"You're adorable." She blows on my clit and licks it once more before sitting up. She shifts us both so I'm slightly on my side. I watch her curiously as she straddles one of my legs and slightly bends the other.

My eyes widen when I figure out what she's doing. We've only scissored one time, but I came so hard, I couldn't move. I'd never done it with anyone before. I think it's one of her favorite things to do. Though, she hasn't exactly said so.

Lyric shuffles herself until her pussy is hovering just over mine. I can feel how wet she is. She doesn't even have to touch me. I can feel her heat when she leans down to kiss me deeply. As she pushes her tongue into my mouth, she drops her clit against mine and starts brushing featherlight against me. I jerk against her, my body begging for more.

She sucks on my tongue as she pulls away and slowly sits up. Her eyes are on me the whole time. She pulls the leg she isn't straddling over her shoulder and presses down harder, giving me the pressure I'm craving.

As if she's torturing me, she moves herself slowly over me. Her clit rubs against mine at the perfect pressure until both of us are moaning and trembling. Thankfully, Lyric can't take the slow pace anymore either and starts thrusting herself over my clit faster.

"Oh... fuck! Yes, Lyric! Yes!" I grip the bed sheets.

Lyric twists her hips as she thrusts over me. Her pussy gets wetter and wetter. Mine feels like it's dripping for her. I push myself against her and meet each and every single one of her thrusts. I watch as her eyes roll back into her head.

"Holy, fuck, Mariah... So good. So good!"

We both thrust against each other faster and harder until I feel the release I've been chasing barreling into me. I grip Lyric's thigh and grind into her as she does me. The tingling deep inside me quickly becomes a raging avalanche. I know I'm not going to last.

"Lyric… Oh my God, I'm going to come…"

"Not yet."

I don't know where the hell she pulled it from, but I feel the tip of one of our vibrators slide into my pussy. "Ah! Lyric! Fuck!" I arch into her and it.

Lyric uses her other hand to help herself drop onto the other side of our dual vibrator. "Oh, fuck… Yes! Yes!" Lyric screams.

"I can't… Lyric… Come! Now! Come for me!"

We scream in pleasure as we both continue to thrust into each other and the vibrator riding out waves and waves of pleasure as our orgasms take over.

But we don't stop.

We continue thrusting against each other while the dual vibrator plunges deep inside both of us. The vibrating sensation inside us, hitting that ever elusive G-spot, drives us both closer and closer to the edge of a second bliss.

I reach up and start rubbing her clit. Lyric follows my lead and does the same to me. We rub each others clits to the pace that we're thrusting over each other and the vibrator. Lyric throws her head back and moans.

"Oh, fuck, Lyric." I flick her clit.

"Ah!" She jerks her hips over mine and flicks my clit in retaliation.

"Lyric! Yes!" I jerk into her, causing the vibrator to sink deeper into us both.

"Mariah… Please… Please!" Lyric's thighs tremble. Her movements become uncontrolled.

"Come, baby. Come for me, my angel. Please, please come for me." I plead with her because I don't want to come without her.

Lyric throws her head back again. "Mariah! Oh, holy fuck, yes! Yes! Mariah!" she screams.

I drop my head back on the pillow and lose total control over myself when I feel her squirt over me, soaking my already wet pussy. "Lyric! Oh God, yes! Lyric, yes!" I scream just as loudly as her, coming at the same time and squirting hard for her, something I've only done a few times, and only ever for her.

After several moments of her laying on top of me and us both panting, we finally decide we should move. Neither of us are a fan of being covered in sweat, but we love laying with each other and cuddling after our love-making.

Lyric blinks as she stands. "Now, how did that get over there?"

I follow her gaze as I stand next to her and giggle. Our vibrator is still on and vibrating on the chair near the window. "You threw it when we came." I kiss her cheek.

Lyric giggles. "You make me lose my mind sometimes when you make me come."

I laugh. "Yeah? I could say the same for you." I kiss her softly before walking to the chair. I shut the toy off and take her hand, leading her to the bathroom to clean the toy and us up. When we're cleaned and dressed, I check the time while I put the vibrator away. "Perfect timing. DJ can't yell at us for being late."

Lyric smiles. "I still can't believe how punctual he is. Even after working with him for so long." She shakes her head. "I mean, Tyler hates when people are late, but DJ is kind of fanatical about it."

"I know. But it's actually something I really like about him. He keeps everyone on track." I link our fingers together as I open the door and run directly into the man I'm speaking of.

Lyric cracks up. "We were literally just talking about you."

DJ grins. "Hopefully, all good things."

"Of course, all good," I tease as we start walking down the hall together. I smile when I see Matt and DJ are holding hands, just as me and Lyric are.

DJ laughs. "Good. You know, I don't know what the fuck made you two scream like that, but you had a little old lady out here about to call ship security. We were just coming back from the pool. You had a nice sized crowd out here."

I look back at him in horror. "You're lying!"

He grins and shakes his head. "Nope. Not even a little bit."

Matt holds out his phone and shows us a video he started playing. Sure as shit, there's a crowd outside our door, and everyone is in shock as they listen to us. Lyric lets out a squeak and shoves his phone back at him before covering her mouth. I just stare in open-mouth shock.

Matt laughs. "For the record, the competition is fucking over. You've definitely won."

I look up at him before turning around to start walking again after taking Lyric's hand. "I didn't know we were still competing."

DJ laughs. "Have you not learned that competitions between us never end? Well, except this one. This one is definitely over. I will concede to you both and hand you the win."

"What the hell made you scream like that anyway?" Matt asks.

Lyric smiles. "One word. Scissoring."

Matt looks at us both in horror. "Like… scissors?" He shakes his head. "Okay, I may be gay, but now I need to know because that sounds fucked up and painful."

"Not with real scissors. Good God. We're not fucking crazy," I say with a laugh as I slap his arm.

Lyric giggles. "We rub our clits together. The position is called scissoring."

Matt rubs his chest. "Thank fuck."

DJ laughs. "We have it easy. It's pretty simple for a guy to get off. We don't have to get into weird fucking positions and end up looking like an octopus. Stick our dicks in, thrust a few times, and done."

"You make it sound so romantic," Lyric quips.

We all laugh as we head for the dining room. I kiss Lyric's hand thinking for the thousandth time since I've met her that I'm so lucky to have found her. Lyric is perfect in every way. She's beautiful. Smart. Creative. Strong. She can hold an intellectual conversation with me like no other, and find plot holes in my books that not even Tyler sees.

But most of all, Lyric is the love of my life.

And all mine.

The End

Bonus Chapter!

Chapter Ten

☆ *Matt* ☆

(The First Day at the MGM Grand in Las Vegas for Mariah's Book Convention)

I look up at the giant hotel in front of me. The MGM Grand. DJ and I have been planning this trip for our anniversary all year. It's the location of Mariah's convention, but also the hotel we've both dreamed of staying in. We've had our room reserved for close to a year.

We've already taken a picture in front of the giant golden lion out front. I can't explain why that excited us. Probably more than the fact that we're staying on the famous Las Vegas strip, and there's a giant casino and multiple five-star restaurants around us and in the hotel itself.

DJ and I walk into the lobby, pulling our luggage behind us. I'm in just as much awe as I was when we walked in here the first time. It's modern. Gorgeous. Pristine.

"Christ," DJ says. "Damn hotel looks like it could be a luxury resort."

"I think it probably is," I chuckle. My eyes fall on Mariah and a very excited woman standing next to her.

"Looks like Lyric and Rih beat us here," DJ says, nodding towards where I'm looking.

"Looks like it." I take out my phone, ready to have a little fun with the girl I've considered my little sister for years. I dial Lyric's phone number.

I watch as she takes out her phone, bouncing a little as she answers. "Matty! It's amazing here! Did you get here? Where are you? Are you here?"

"Well, we did just arrive, but there's this chick in front of us who's bouncing like she's going to pop right off Earth and head right for space. Damn good thing the woman holding her hand is keeping her on the ground."

I grin as she starts looking around with a confused expression. "Where?"

"She's wearing a purple tank top and short as fuck shorts." I wink at DJ when he barks out a laugh.

She squeaks. "She is not wearing what I am! Well, minus the short shorts." She looks down at her outfit. "Okay, maybe they are a little short. But it's really hot!"

"Well, I don't know what you're wearing, but the girl next to her is wearing shorts even shorter than hers. Practically show her ass cheeks. And the pink tank is tight. Shows off all the curves she has and more. If I weren't gay, I'd be all over that."

I grin as her entire posture changes. I know she's caught on as she looks around for me. "You asshole. You see me and Mariah."

I crack up. "Is that who I see?"

She finally turns towards the door and sees DJ bent over holding his sides and me grinning like the asshole I really am. "I hate you." She hangs up with a teasing pout.

I grin and wave as I hang up my phone. "Hey, girls!"

Mariah laughs as they both bounce-walk over to us holding hands. Lyric throws her arms around me. Mariah throws hers around DJ. Then they switch. It's lucky our anniversary ended up being the same weekend as this convention. Mariah was booked for it at the last minute. Considering how cooped up the two have been over the past couple of weeks since the 9/11 Memorial tour, this convention is an amazing reprieve.

And DJ and I feel a lot better being here with them. We've found out a lot of things that we haven't shared with either of them. Like how Justice's boyfriend was lying about his identity. He's really Blake Ericson, a Sergeant with Gainesville P.D. who works under me and DJ. He's also Lyric's partner. We've never been so happy to have Lyric away from this shit. We refuse to tell her what we've found out, though, because it would break her. She likes her partner a lot. Fuck. Most of the department does.

"Oh!" Mariah says as she takes out her phone. "I know you guys said you have a room and it's fine, but Tyler upgraded your room to one of the penthouses. He said it's next to ours."

DJ shakes his head with a chuckle. "You didn't need to, but thank you."

"I know. But Tyler has ways. And Lyric and I wanted to do something nice for you for your anniversary. So, the penthouse is part of it. The other thing is the helicopter tour of Hoover Dam. I know Matt really wanted to do that."

I smile. "I did. But I sacrificed it for the actual ground tour for DJ."

"Well." Mariah shrugs. "Now you get both. And an awesome penthouse, courtesy of Alexander Publishing House."

DJ laughs. "Hell, I'll take it. I saw pictures of the penthouses while we were booking our room. I almost reserved one, but they were booked."

Lyric giggles, probably knowing the strings that had to have been pulled to get us the suite. "Now you have one."

"But if anyone asks, you're part of Mariah Marie's security team," Tyler says, coming up to us with his nose in his phone. He hands us all keycards to our room. I raise an eyebrow and glance at DJ when Tyler doesn't look up at us but continues talking. "Both suites are ready. Take the private elevator up. It says penthouse. You can't access it without a special card which will also open your rooms. If you need me, I'll be grabbing the schedule for your speech tomorrow night and setting up the booth for this weekend. We need to market your new book." He looks at his watch. "Dinner for the five of us and your two security guards at seven.

Meet at Crush." He walks off towards wherever they are holding the convention without glancing up at any of us for even a second.

"Well, that was a little intimidating," DJ says, staring after him. "He just dictates everything without looking up?"

Lyric cracks up. "DJ, seriously? You do that. Tyler is literally a younger, less hot version of you."

DJ grins. "You think I'm hot?" He winks. "Sorry, sweetheart. I'm taken," he drawls, exaggerating his Texas accent and putting his arm around me, pulling him close to his side. I let out a low groan. I'll never get tired of his accent. I don't know what it is about it, but it drives me fucking crazy.

Mariah laughs. "So is she." She tugs Lyric possessively to her side. I know she's teasing, but it still makes Lyric blush. "You'll have to fight me for her."

I laugh. "I don't think we would want to fight you. If you're anything like your girl, you probably fight fucking dirty. I happen to like my dick. And DJ's, too." I wiggle my eyebrows, causing everyone to laugh.

"What do you say to going upstairs?" DJ asks quietly as Lyric leans in and whispers something in Mariah's ear.

"Holy fuck, yes," I hoarsely say as quietly as possible. DJ's jade eyes mirror my own desire to have him close to me, inside me, and any other way he wants to give me.

We lead the girls to the elevator for the penthouse level. I love them both to death, but they are the last thing on my mind right now. The only thing I can think of is DJ's hand brushing against my dick while no one is watching. Except Mariah's security, but I doubt they're paying us any mind. Not with the way their eyes are protectively swiveling the lobby. Good thing because my cock is hard as a rock. I'm going to have to use DJ to hide it.

Thankfully, the elevator ride is quiet and quick. Mariah's security guards pay us no attention. I'm sure they've seen and heard more than their fair share of sexual shit. They're probably really good at ignoring it at this point and just doing their jobs.

I laugh as Lyric and Mariah follow us out into the hall. I don't know what Mariah did, but Lyric is blushing and looks like she's about ready to pounce on Mariah right here in the hall. "Have fun, you two!" I wink.

Lyric blushes an even more furious shade of red, nearly running after Mariah's sudden speed walk. She doesn't get a chance to look back at me, but it doesn't stop her smart-ass remark. "As if you ain't gonna be bent over for DJ within seconds of closing the door! Try not to be loud. I don't need to hear my brothers fucking."

DJ cracks up. "The girl ain't wrong. Try not to scream my name too loudly."

I laugh as DJ's hand squeezes mine. "Well, now I'll be fucking sure to!"

Mariah opens the door for her and Lyric as Lyric giggles. DJ pulls me into our room as security disappears into the girl's room to check it out. We take a second to look around our room, but it's while DJ is pulling me to our bedroom.

The floor to ceiling window spans the entire sitting room and shows off the best of the Las Vegas strip. The plush couch and oversized chair are pure white. Inviting. There's a kitchenette if we don't want to leave the room or want room service.

As soon as we get to the bedroom, DJ has me pushed against a wall and is kissing me with a ferocity I don't get much from him. I love when he does it, but losing control isn't DJ's style. When he does give it up, it's the sexiest fucking thing I've ever seen.

I tangle my fingers in his hair and tug while I nip and suck on his tongue. He groans and pushes his erection against me as he pulls my belt from the loops on my jeans and tosses it somewhere. He undoes the button and zipper lightning quick and pushes my jeans down while he's turning me around.

His teeth against my shoulder and his hands against my abs while he lifts my shirt makes my dick harden even more. The shirt gets tossed, and I'm once again pressed against the wall. I'm not sure I can take him not being inside me much longer. He doesn't leave me waiting. DJ never leaves me waiting.

"Holy fuck, DJ!" I yell loudly as I groan. His large and thick cock fills me in one sure thrust. I immediately clench around him. He stays still, even though he's seated deep inside me. "Fuck," I groan as my hand reaches back to grip him, knocking something off the nightstand near the bed. It crashes to the ground. I don't even care.

DJ starts thrusting into me hard. Holding onto his hip with one hand, I reach down to protect my dick from slamming against the wall. I'm just as big as he is, maybe a little more. Slamming my cock into a wall is painful as fuck.

Reading me, DJ stops thrusting. "Bed," he commands. Without pulling out, he walks us back to the bed and bends me over the end of it. "Fuck, I love the way you feel around me."

I brace myself on the bed as he bends over me. He runs his teeth and tongue along my shoulder blades. I hiss at the sensation as goosebumps erupt in the wake of his mouth. He starts thrusting hard and deep once more.

He's hard and thick. Just the way I like him. He grips my dick and starts jerking it in time to his thrusts. "Fucking hell, DJ!" I yell.

DJ grips my hips as he stands. "Have I told you lately how fucking good you feel?" He doesn't stop the grueling, hard pace he's set as he pounds deep into my ass.

I clench around him as I moan, taking all of him again and again. I grip the blanket underneath me. "Yes. But fuck, tell me again."

He slaps my ass with a hiss when I tighten. "So fucking good, baby."

The headboard is slamming against the wall so hard, I fear it might break, but when DJ rolls his hips against mine and hits just the right spot, I forget everything except him. I moan as my eyes roll back into my head. I collapse on the bed, unable to hold myself up anymore.

"Fuck, DJ. Don't stop..." I'm close to the edge. The release my dick has been begging for ever since we left Gainesville and boarded the plane to come here is almost upon me. It's not my fault my husband is so damn gorgeous. I always want him.

"I didn't plan to." He pounds into me again and again, but when he slams into me and buries himself in me, I see stars.

"Come. Now. I can feel you need to."

"Fuck, I'll make a damn mess." I grit my teeth and force myself not to, so I don't fuck up the bedspread underneath me.

I can feel DJ grinning. I know I fucked up. "Then don't. You can come in me." He says nothing else. He squeezes my dick just tight enough to cut off any chance I have of coming. He comes hard inside me as he starts to thrust once more so hard that the headboard begins slamming into the wall again.

"Mariah!" Lyric screams. The headboard from their bed slams into the wall as ours does. I'm surprised as hell the wall hasn't given with all the pounding against it. "Fuck! Mariah! I'm coming! It's coming!"

I grin but have no chance to react before DJ gives me one last hard thrust, shoving me into the bed harder than I already am. "Holy fuck, DJ!" I scream as the entire fucking bed slams against the wall hard enough to shake it.

"Hey, you guys! You might end up coming through the wall next time!" Mariah yells as she laughs.

"Round one goes to us!" DJ yells back.

I look back at him incredulously. "Did you seriously just do that to win this competition?"

"You know how competitive things get between us all." He winks as he pulls out.

I laugh as I stand slowly. "My turn."

"You think you can win us round two?"

I raise an eyebrow. "You've said it yourself. I'm the best fuck you've ever had. It's why you married me." I grin teasingly, knowing that isn't the only reason.

DJ laughs as he finishes stripping. I can't help but feel proud of myself for the fact that he wanted me so much, he hadn't even finished undressing before he was inside me. His jeans were undone enough for him to get his dick out, and that's all. I love when he loses at least a fraction of the control he loves so much.

I lay on my back on the bed and wait for him to straddle me. I grip his hips with a grin as I look up at him. DJ is by far more dominant than I am. While I'll let him bend me over or fuck me against a wall, he has never allowed me to do that to him. DJ likes being on top. Even if it is my dick in his ass, I don't have as much control over anything as he does. It works, though. I'm content with the amount of control he gives up to me.

DJ lowers himself over me and moans as he takes me deep into him. We both close our eyes with low sighs. My fingertips dig into his ass. His fall to my stomach and trace my abs before gripping my hips. I open my eyes and wait for him to settle before I start thrusting.

Hard, deep, and at the same punishing pace he did.

"Jesus mother of fuck! Matt!" DJ yells loudly. It doesn't take the bed long to start creaking under us and hitting the wall. I'm sure we'll have a damage fee to pay.

"My God! Did you switch? How are you old men handling this?" Lyric yells through the wall. I'm forty. DJ is fifty. Lyric is ten years younger than me, but her favorite fucking thing to do is call us old.

The teasing causes us both to crack up. "Shut up and fuck your girl, you brat!" I yell back. I don't stop thrusting into DJ for a second. If anything, I thrust harder, deeper, rolling my hips.

"Holy fuck!" DJ yells. Something crashes to the ground again. I look over and see the picture that was above the nightstand on the ground.

"Don't mind if I do!" Lyric calls back, giggling.

DJ groans as he tightens around me, looking at the framed picture that is now shattered. "We'll have to pay for that."

I can hear Mariah laugh. "This is going to be a long night," she says.

"She has no idea," DJ says. He starts bouncing on my dick harder and faster, twisting his hips.

I drop my head back on the pillows. "Jesus Christ. So fucking good," I groan. I'm dangerously close to losing it, but I don't want to yet. DJ isn't ready, and one of my favorite things is when he comes on my stomach.

So, I keep thrusting, rocking my hips against his ass as he rides my cock, tightening around me with each and every thrust I give him.

"Oh! Ah! Lyric!" Mariah screams.

"Oh fuck, Matt," DJ groans leaning back and taking me even deeper.

"Oh, fuck me," I grind out through gritted teeth when I sink even further into him.

"Lyric! Holy shit! I'm gonna come. It's coming! I'm coming!" Mariah screams. "Fuck! Yes!"

"Matt, holy shit," DJ moans, clenching tight around me. I grip his dick before he can and start stroking him in time with my thrusts.

"Ah!" Mariah screams, making both DJ and I jerk our heads towards the wall. "Ah!" she screams again. "Lyric! Fuck, yes!"

I don't have any time to make a smart-ass comment, though, because the familiar tingling at the base of my spine surges through my stomach and directly to my cock. I stroke faster, firmer. I know I'm not holding out much longer.

"Fuck, DJ, I'm gonna come."

"Me, too. Come for me. Now."

"Oh, yes, DJ," I groan, giving him one last thrust and burying my cock deep inside him as I give him the release I've been waiting for. My hips jerk up into his as I hold him still.

He comes at the same time as me. "Oh, fuck yes, Matt!" DJ yells as I jerk his dick. I let out a satiated moan, feeling his come spurt onto me.

He collapses on me, still connected with me at the most intimate of levels, while we catch our breath. I wrap my arms around him, not caring for a second his come is on my hand or me. I hug him tightly while we come down.

"We should probably get cleaned up," I say after a few moments.

DJ glances at the clock. "Probably. I'd hate to go up against the drill sergeant Mariah calls her agent."

I laugh. "You love it. He's just like you."

"A younger, less hot version, I'm told." He grins as I pull out, and he gets up.

"The girl speaks the truth, even if she was just teasing."

DJ laughs as he helps me up and leads me to the bathroom. "We made quite the mess. I can feel my fucking come on my back."

I grin. "Don't worry. I'll lick it off." I lean in and lick his shoulder just to prove my point.

"While I wouldn't mind, we do have somewhere to be." He wets down a couple of washcloths and puts soap on them before handing me one and turning around so I can wash the come off his back.

Lyric slaps the wall hard. "Guess what, Matty? I just made my girl squirt!"

I laugh. "I guess we know where those screams came from."

DJ grins as we clean ourselves. "I think we'll have to call that one a win for them."

"That ties us up. We can't leave this at a tie."

DJ laughs as he turns around and rinses off his cloth. "What the fuck is wrong with us? Are we really that competitive that we're competing sexually with two girls we consider family just to prove we're better in bed and can scream louder?"

I shrug with a smile and rinse off my cloth when we're done. "Can't say we're boring."

DJ laughs and leans in. He kisses me with a low moan. "I don't think anyone would say we're boring."

I smile against his lips, giving him a last peck before leading him out of the bathroom. We both get dressed in one of the nicer outfits we brought because neither of us know what to expect from this restaurant we're going to.

After we're dressed, I slap the wall. "Round two goes to you," I say. "No fucking way I could top those screams. We'll call it a draw."

DJ and I both laugh when we hear them both laugh. DJ holds out a hand. "Ready to celebrate our anniversary with those that mean the world to us?"

I smile and take his hand. "More than ready."

But most of all, I'm happy as hell I'm celebrating an anniversary I never thought I'd have with the one person in the world who holds my heart.

Next In The Beautiful Dream Series

The sweet and sinfully sexy Beautiful Dream Series continues with
Ravishing Our Queen.

I'm perfectly content letting people believe what they want about me, but it's not easy being a high-ranking officer in law enforcement who is bisexual.

Luckily, I found someone who shares my sexuality and attitude about it being no one's business.

Captain DJ Rens. My partner and best friend.

We have each other. We have jobs with the Gainesville Police Department that we both love. And when we need to scratch our itch to share a woman, we head directly to our favorite club, Sapphire's, a club filled with the type of women we long for. When it's over, we send them on their way.

That is until the one night that changes our lives forever.

We'll never be the same. Not after having a taste of *her*. The only women we've ever wanted to stay. To be *ours*.

But we don't have a chance to explore the possibilities she promises because we are violently thrown into a dark world of secrets and lies that we must unravel.

Because it's not only lives at risk this time…

It's our hearts.

Order ***Ravishing Our Queen*** Today!

The Beautiful Dream Series

Available Now

Loving You
My Love, My Heart
Softening Lyric
Undercover Temptations
Captain Charming
Breaking Boundaries
Crashing Into You
Tactical Inferno
Ravishing Our Queen
Cherished By The Texan
Unveiling Our Passions

Box Sets Available

The Beautiful Dream Series: Box Set: Part 1
The Beautiful Dream Series: Box Set: Part 2

Other Books By Melony Ann

The Crane Family Series

Available Now

The Reluctant Mafia King
Sweet Lies
Billion Dollar Love Story
Be Mine
Protecting Her
Dangerously Forbidden Love
His Heart
Love In The Dark

Box Sets Available

The Crane Family Series

The Deimos Trilogy

Available Now

Connor's Legacy
Aryan's Alpha
Kade's Redemption

Box Sets Available

The Deimos Trilogy

The Forbidden Temptation Series

Available Now

The Detective's Forbidden Temptation
The Running Back's Forbidden Temptation

The Lucinio Family Series

Available Now

Rising From The Ashes
The Player's Rebel
Encrypting My Heart
Fighting My Fate

Multi Author Series
Piper Falls: Firehouse 49

Available Now

Ignite My Fire by Melony Ann
Regain My Fire by Kindra White
Playing With My Fire by D.L. Howe
Fight My Fire by Darley Collins
Against My Fire by Anneke Boshoff
Relight My Fire by Louise Murchie
Harness My Fire by Ayana Lisbet
Quench My Fire by Havana Wilder

Let's Be Friends

Follow me on

Bookbub

Facebook

Goodreads

Instagram

Tik Tok

Visit my website
www.melonyannauthor.com

Subscribe to my newsletter and get a FREE never-seen-before NOVELLA
just for subscribers!
https://www.melonyannauthor.com/exclusive-content

Join my Facebook Reader Group!
Melony Ann's Sizzling Book Nook
https://www.facebook.com/groups/melonyannssizzlingbooknook

The official Beautiful Dream Series Playlist on YouTube
https://youtube.com/playlist?list=PLGEiD5wbQmDe1z4_FeeKbMLcBkOz
1M4L4

Dedication

To our entire universe. The amazing men and little men who are always by our side. We love you with a depth that is scary; a strength that is unyielding.

Acknowledgements

Brad - When my world goes crazy, you're the sturdy structure in the wind keeping me safe from the wreckage. You're my safe harbor, and I love you.

Laura - You're the fire in my veins that warms the ice. You're my entire world, and I love you so very much, my angel.

Jay - Some heroes don't wear capes. For the last God only knows how many years, you've been my hero. Ever since you saved me from the Duluth airport chaos and stuck with me all through Detroit. I love you.

Anneke - You've become such an integral part of my world over the past couple of years. You're honestly one of my best friends, but also so much more. I can't wait until you're stateside. It's been such a long road. I'm so happy you're in my life.

Jason - This can be your first FF romance. You're welcome.

Kayla - You know when I get to the point where I'm going to simply blow up? Thank you for being the one who lets me scream until I'm calm again.

To the Bookstagram Community.

To my family.

To all of those who believe in me and support me.

To all of those who don't.

Cover by: Carter Cover Designs

Edited by: Alyssa Skaggs

About Melony Ann

Melony Ann began writing short stories and poetry as a child. She continued honing her craft over the years until she took the plunge and began publishing her work, despite having severe anxiety.

Melony writes contemporary romance stories that are full of suspense and a lot of steam.

When she isn't writing, she is loving her family and working to make her life something she deserves.

Melony believes that if her writing can inspire just one person, then all of her hard work is worth it.

Her hope is that her writing allows each and every one of her readers to escape for a little while. To dive into a different world one book at a time.

www.ingramcontent.com/pod-product-compliance
Lightning Source LLC
Chambersburg PA
CBHW071923220626
47052CB00002B/437